DISPLACED PERSON

Marie Halun Bloch

DISPLACED PERSON

decorations by ALLEN DAVIS

LOTHROP, LEE & SHEPARD COMPANY

A Division of William Morrow & Co., Inc. • New York

Text copyright © 1978 by Marie Halun Bloch
Illustrations copyright © 1978 by Allen Davis
Printed in the United States of America.
First Edition
1   2   3   4   5   6   7   8   9   10

Library of Congress Cataloging in Publication Data
Bloch, Marie Halun.
    Displaced person.

    SUMMARY: Fourteen-year-old Stefan, a Ukrainian refugee, struggles to
survive as a displaced person in Nazi Germany during the final days of
World War II.
    1. World War, 1939–1945—Germany—Juvenile fiction.   2. World War,
1939–1945—Ukraine—Juvenile fiction.   3. Ukraine—History—German
occupation, 1941–1944—Juvenile fiction.   [1. World War, 1939–1945—
Germany—Fiction.   2. World War, 1939–1945—Ukraine—Fiction.
3. Ukraine—History—German occupation, 1941–1944—Fiction.   4. World
War, 1939–1945—Refugees—Fiction.   5. Refugees—Fiction]   I. Davis, Allen.
II. Title.
PZ7.B6194Di   [Fic]   78-13083
ISBN 0-688-41860-0   ISBN 0-688-51860-5 lib. bdg.

For DONALD BEATY BLOCH

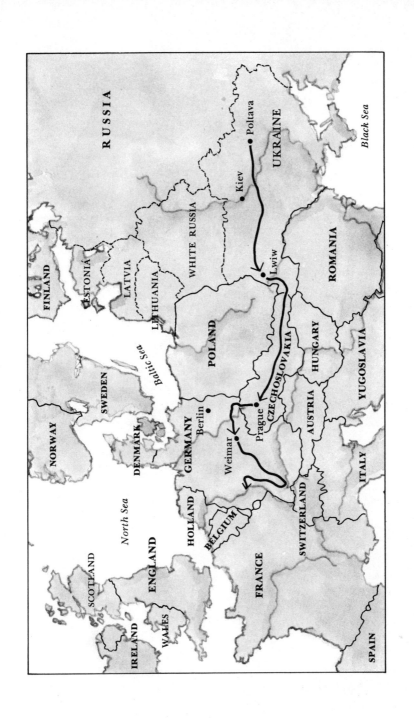

one

STEFAN DROPPED HIS PACK INTO THE BOTTOM BUNK and, without waiting for word from anyone, climbed in right after it. His bones ached so that he could hardly get himself into it. The thin mattress rustled beneath him as he lay down atop the coarse blanket.

He closed his eyes to shut out the sight of strangers and covered his exposed ear with his hand to shut out the babble of voices. But the voices came crowding in for all that, creating a jangle of noise in his head. And the smell. The smell was the smell of all humanity, of the smoke of cheap tobacco, of wet wool, of strong disinfectant and pesticide.

He opened his eyes for an instant but, when he caught sight of the black cloth over the single window, he shuddered and closed them again.

Then he began to shiver. The shivering came

9

from deep within and, try as he would, he could not stop it but lay shaking, teeth chattering.

Out of the jumble of noises, one voice spoke out. "What's the matter with your boy? See to him! He may be ill."

It was a woman's voice, speaking Ukrainian.

Now hands were helping to peel off his wet clothes and get him under the blanket. They tucked it in all around him. Though the blanket did not stop the shivering, the feel of it wrapping him like a snug cocoon was a comfort—a shield from the January cold, from the dismal room and the chaos, the everlasting chaos, from the hopeless wandering and the everlasting good-bys. . . .

Then somebody made him sit up and drink something hot. It might have been tea, but it tasted odd. He turned his face away. "Drink it!" his father's voice commanded. "It's only water."

The last he knew that night someone—a man's voice—was saying, "When the Americans come . . . when the Americans come . . . come . . . come . . ."

Long afterward, as if in answer, a woman's voice said, "No, we can't stay here."

Stefan opened his eyes at these words, spoken quietly.

"No, we can't stay here," the voice repeated. "Bedbugs. Perhaps worse. I didn't sleep the whole night long."

Stefan lay on his side without stirring, listening, wondering vaguely where he was, already knowing that, wherever it was, he did not want to be there.

He must have slept a long time—through the night —for his mouth felt dry and bitter from heavy sleep.

Not far above his head, from the corner of his eye, he saw the bottom of the bunk above. Shifting his gaze to the bunk across the narrow aisle, he saw a lump huddled under a blanket. Perhaps it was not a person but something hidden under the blanket. He stared at it. It did not move. It did not seem to be breathing. A feeling of panic began to steal through him. But with an effort he managed to suppress it and gradually it vanished.

"We must leave at once . . . today . . . in search of another place," the woman's voice continued.

"And what will we pay with? Tell me that." A man's voice.

"We'll offer to work. I'll cook. You . . . ."

A short laugh, more of a snort. "By now they're up to their ears in cheap labor here. The Nazis have got all Europe laboring for them, for a bowl of thin soup once a day. Do you think they'll need you to cook for them?"

At these words, so outspoken, Stefan came further awake. That was it. They were in the very heart of Germany by now—somewhere near the old city of Weimar—in a barracks or hostel of some sort. Everyone seemed to be still asleep, except for the man and woman talking quietly somewhere nearby and a child in a far corner crying fretfully. Behind him someone was snoring heavily. But snores were coming from all over the barracks.

Then someone—he did not see who—pulled back

the black cloth over the window, letting in the gray beginning of the winter's day. Stefan lifted himself up on his elbow and looked. Then, feeling weak, he let himself fall back onto the mattress, glad that he did not have to get up.

Now, all over the crowded room, people began stirring. Groans. Coughing. Reluctant voices hoarse with sleep.

No sooner had Stefan settled down again to go back to sleep than he felt a bite on his leg. He rubbed his other foot against it. But now he felt one on his chest.

Flinging back the blanket, he sat up, lifted his undershirt and looked. Sure enough, there it was, small, oval, and rather flat. And it was feeding on him. With a grunt of disgust he brushed the thing off.

"You should kill it first," a voice spoke from across the aisle.

Stefan glanced over. It was a boy in the middle bunk of the neighboring tier, older than himself by a year or two probably. He had a well-shaped head, straight dark hair, and his full lips wore a pleasant, self-possessed expression, oddly out of keeping with the surroundings. "Otherwise," he went on, "it'll just move onto someone else."

"I never . . ." Stefan began.

"I know. Me neither . . . except for a place in Poland."

Stefan lay down again. But the boy continued. "What's your name?" he asked.

12

Stefan neither stirred nor looked at him. "Stefan," he said at last. But he refrained from asking the question in his turn.

No matter. The boy supplied the answer all the same. "That's odd," he said. "My last name is Stefanyk. My first is Martin."

He and his mother had been on the road, Martin said, for almost nine months. Stefan did not bother to tell him that he and his father had left home more than a year ago and in successive stages had traveled, mostly on foot, all the way from Poltava in eastern Ukraine, westward across the breadth of Ukraine, then across Slovakia—

He and his mother, Martin was now saying, were from Ternopil in western Ukraine, a region that had been taken over by the Soviets for the first time only six years before. At the takeover, in 1939, his father had been imprisoned for "anti-Soviet agitation." But two years later, he and his fellow prisoners were murdered, right there in the prison, by the Soviet Army when it was forced to beat a retreat before the onslaught of the Wehrmacht, the invading German Army. "That way they didn't have to bother with taking prisoners along on the retreat," Martin explained, his dark eyes suddenly large and staring.

Stefan gave him a look. What was this kid telling him all this for? As if he needed an explanation of how and why the Soviets disposed of their prisoners! He could tell this kid a thing or two himself, if he wanted to take the trouble. . . .

Martin and his mother, who was a librarian by

13

profession, were traveling with an old woman who came from the region of Kiev, the capital of Ukraine. Martin pointed to the bunk just above Stefan's. "Everyone calls her Granny Sophia," he explained. "We picked her up after her old man was hanged by the Germans." He paused, and then added thoughtfully, "He was just an ordinary old man, you know."

Martin recounted all this as if he had been asked for his life history and that of his neighbors.

One could tell such people easily—those who at some time or other had lived in the West, in regions that had not been subjected to long Soviet rule, as had been much of Ukraine and other nations in the Soviet Union. Such people were more open, did not seem to be hiding something, spoke freely with strangers and all others alike in an animated way that was quite different from the guarded, deliberate, thoughtful manner of nearly everyone that Stefan had ever known. In a word, dynamite, dangerous to associate with. Stay away from them.

All the same, "West" was a magic word that conjured up all kinds of visions, all kinds of feelings.

At school in Poltava "the West" had meant the conglomeration of capitalist nations, such as England and France, Canada and the United States, and the rest. Most of all the United States.

"Lydia, describe capitalism."

Lydia had stood stiffly at her desk in the prescribed manner and, as if reciting from memory, in a voice that matched her undersized frame, she had reeled off: "Under capitalism, one, the bosses own the means of production. Two, they exploit the workers. So the workers starve while the few capitalists live in idleness and luxury. Three . . . in general . . . in general the ruling class exploits the workers and—and—it's not very nice. . . ."

Someone in the back of the room tittered.

The teacher's glance flew in that direction. "It's no laughing matter," she had said sharply.

In the precarious seclusion of home, on the other hand, "the West" had meant a fairyland of freedom, a country where one was free to speak one's thoughts —and in one's own tongue, what's more—free to write and proclaim one's ideas, to move about freely, to practice one's religion. A fabled place.

Not that Stefan's parents had ever said any of this to him. But just from stray words dropped now and again, from certain looks and gestures, even from certain silences he had formed such a vision.

But here was this Martin, still talking, nonstop. "Do you know where you're going?" he asked.

Stefan only shook his head.

"Neither do we," Martin said.

They looked at each other mutely for a moment, and then Martin laughed softly.

As if it were a laughing matter.

Stefan looked away. He did not shut his eyes but lay eyeing the bunk directly opposite. The lump huddled under the blanket had not stirred all this while. Again, and more forcibly this time, the shape of it struck him as odd.

As he stared, the realization at last came to him

that that was the same bunk his father had taken the night before. With that, in one motion Stefan leaped out of bed, pulled away the blanket in the bunk, and revealed a valise with a rope tied around it. In a panic, swaying a little from his weakness, he looked swiftly around.

Martin was watching from above. "Your dad's gone," he said, "to Weimar. He'll be back."

Chagrined at having been caught so unnerved, Stefan turned and crept back into his bunk, the better to hide from the world.

. . . one may be screaming inside in panic or pain, anger or fear, but one's face shows only a pleasant expression, the eyes bright and eager, the corners of the lips upturned. Laugh? Of course! One may laugh one's head off! Laughter is the best mask of all. The more one laughs, the more people are put off.

This was not something his mother had taught him—and certainly not his father. They were rules that he had formed, almost unconsciously, by himself, simply by breathing his native air. Yet here he was among these strangers breaking the first rule of existence.

From the topmost bunk of Martin's tier, a woman was making her way down, dressed in a skirt and blouse. "Here's my mother," Martin said. "Everyone calls her Mrs. Natalia." He laughed. "Except me, of course. She likes the top bunk because it's more private."

Reaching the floor, the woman turned to Stefan. "Good! You're feeling better."

16

It was the voice he had heard through his chills and fever the night before. Approaching Stefan, Mrs. Natalia reached down, placed a cool hand on his brow, and stood gazing speculatively at him. She had dark hair, like Martin, and her eyes were large, dark, and luminous. "Evidently no fever this morning," she said, taking her hand away. "Your father," she went on, "went back to Weimar very early this morning to find a better place to stay."

"He told me to watch his valise," Martin put in, pointing to it.

At this, for some perverse reason, Stefan felt a sting of something like jealousy. He looked at the boy. "Thanks," he said, with a smile, "but I'll take care of it now."

"Oh, it's no trouble," Martin said, cheerily.

Stefan eyed him, the smile still on his face. That's all you know about it, brother.

"Get dressed, Martin," Mrs. Natalia said. "Go get your ration of soup while there's still some to be had."

And with that she left. A few minutes later Martin was ready to follow her. "I'll bring you back some bread if you want," he said.

"No . . . no, thanks," Stefan replied. "There's some in our pack."

"See you later, then," Martin said, and with an easy wave of his hand he was gone.

Stefan settled back in the bunk and closed his eyes. In the growing hum of talk around him, besides Ukrainian, he could hear snatches of Russian, Polish—

and two languages he could not identify. Perhaps they were Latvian or Esthonian. Maybe Lithuanian. All of them war refugees, like himself and his father.

The bedbugs had by now crawled back into their hiding places for the day. Several times Stefan almost drowsed off. But the thought that he must guard the valise would not let him sleep.

At last he flung back his blanket again and swung his legs over the edge of the bunk. He sat for a moment, gathering strength, then began to put on his clothes. They were still a little damp from yesterday's tramp from Weimar through the snowstorm, but his body heat would soon dry them completely.

When he had dressed, he sat on the edge of his father's bunk across the way, not knowing what to do with himself. The old woman called Granny Sophia had not yet stirred in the bunk above his. Stefan glanced around at some of the other tiers. Most of their occupants were already gone.

As Stefan sat there, the thought of food began to grow less distasteful. At least some soup might still the rumbling of his stomach and remedy his light-headedness. He had lied to Martin: there was no food in their pack. His last meal had been on the train that had brought them into Germany from Prague. Was that really only the night before last? It seemed a world away. The remembrance of that meal only served to increase his hunger now.

But there was the valise. He did not know what to do. He glanced about, half in search of someone who would tell him.

At this moment, the old woman in the bunk above his stirred. Legs appeared over the edge as she sat up. Taking no notice of him, she made the sign of the cross and shut her eyes. Then her lips began to move. Stefan stared. At last it came to him. "She's praying!" he said to himself.

Half in shock at the sight, Stefan continued to stare. He could not remember having ever before seen a person in prayer. Certainly not in public! At school they had been constantly warned that such a practice was backward, superstitious, "not cultured." As a matter of fact, it was forbidden to teach a child to pray or to take him to church. Watching the old woman, Stefan half expected someone to come rushing up and jeer at her, the way members of the Komsomol—the Young Communist League—had done at church-goers at home.

At home, though his mother had occasionally attended church, she had done so furtively, so that the neighbors would not find out and report her. If word had reached the authorities that she was attending church, she would have lost her good job at once.

As for himself, one time his Pioneer troop had been taken on an excursion to one of the churches that had been converted to a "museum of atheism." Afterward, he could remember nothing of the museum. But of the church itself—the magnificent wall paintings bigger than life, the gorgeous mosaic pictures on the walls, so fine that they looked like oil paintings—of these he had kept a vivid memory to this very day.

Now the old woman was crossing herself again. She opened her eyes. Seeing Stefan watching her, she said, "Aha, so you're feeling better. Well, heaven be thanked! Now you ought to go have something to eat, child. Not that it's much. But you ought to go."

"I can't, Granny. I have to watch my father's valise."

"Do you really think someone will take it?" the old woman asked. "I'll watch it for you, if it comes to that."

Stefan hesitated. To be rid of it! But then he said, "Thanks, Granny. But I'll just take it along."

"Very well," the old woman said, "however you wish."

She climbed down from bunk and with slow steps made her way down the aisle. As soon as she was out of sight, Stefan stood and lifted the valise out of his father's bunk. On second thought, he put it down again. Stepping across to his own bunk, he reached for his pack. With his body carefully screening it, he undid it, and took out a bar of soap still in its fancy square box of red and gilt. He stuffed it into his pocket, refastened the pack, and shoved it into a corner of the bunk.

The valise in hand again, with a wobbly gait he started down the aisle. From within their bunks people turned their heads and stared, first at him and then at the valise, as he went hobbling by. He did not change his expression, but inside he felt hot embarrassment over the attention focused upon him— all on account of that cursed valise.

two

AT THE BARRACKS DOOR AT LAST, STEFAN STEPPED
out into pale, tremulous winter sunshine. The first
thing that caught his eye was the high wire fence
around the compound. He stood mesmerized by the
barbed wire strung all along the top of it. As he
stared, he could feel the pounding of his heart thumping in his ears.

Then he noticed that at the gate stood a guard, a
German, apparently, well past middle age. Evidently,
he was supposed to check the passes of people leaving the compound, but plenty of those going through
the gate neglected to present theirs and the old man
did not bother to hail them back.

Stefan took a deep breath and relaxed. Looking
about now, he saw that their refuge was a typical
army barracks, cheerless and severely featureless, the
buildings ranged like faceless marching men. Prob-

21

ably the Wehrmacht units that had once occupied it had gone to war on the eastern front, in the Soviet Union, and had not been replaced. Perhaps there were no longer even any young men to replace them.

Just within the gate stood the small box of a building where, the night before, Stefan's father had registered them as in need of refuge. People were crisscrossing the big bare yard in front of the barracks, while some went streaming out of the gate and down the road. Others, tin mug in hand, were hurrying toward a barracks to the right from which a line stretched for a short distance across the yard. Many, Stefan saw, were wearing armbands on which, in large black letters, were printed the letters OST. He puzzled over that as he made his way toward the queue, wondering what it meant. Those wearing the armbands—boys and girls alike—seemed to be only a little older than himself.

Reaching the queue, he took his place behind a tall thin man and set down the valise at last. As he stood working his numbed hand, the man turned and, glancing first at Stefan and then at the valise said, "Don't expect them to fill that with food for you, my boy!"

Several in the line, turning to look, laughed. Though Stefan felt his face redden, he managed a laugh, too. Inwardly, however, he felt sudden anger. Must he suffer ridicule over the valise as well?

As he stood struggling with himself, a faint drone caught his ear. He glanced quickly at the people in line. They had not stirred. Hadn't they heard?

As the drone grew steadily louder, Stefan felt the familiar thumping in his ears begin again. He stood stock-still for a long moment. Then he grabbed up the valise and broke away from the line. He ran blindly, not picking any direction. But, burdened with the valise, he felt as though he were running hobbled—as in a frightful dream he had once had in which he ran and ran through heavy billows, but never moved from the spot.

All at once, a hand fell upon his shoulder. "Hold on!" a voice commanded. "There's nowhere to run!" It was the tall thin man again.

"Let go!" Stefan shook himself loose.

But the man grabbed him again. "Wait!" he said. "There's nowhere to run. Believe me, there's nowhere. So come back."

Stefan suddenly slackened, stopped struggling, and allowed himself to be led back into line. No one had stirred from his place and, to Stefan's relief, everyone refrained from looking at him, as if they were ashamed of something, too. But maybe he had done exactly what they really wanted to do: run. Only they couldn't because they were grown-ups.

The planes were nearly overhead now. Stefan stood quite still, waiting. He did not dare to shut his eyes, for then he would see again the ditch by the roadside filled with people huddled into the earth, fountains of dirt shooting skyward all around them, and himself lying in the ditch with the others, flesh tensed, head splitting from the whine and burst of bombs.

Here they come. Stefan stood drowning in the roar.

When he came to, the man was looking soberly down at him. Drawing a deep breath, Stefan dared at last to look skyward. The skies were empty.

The man stooped and picked up the valise. Stefan suddenly came alive. "No, no!" he cried. "I'll take it!"

The man gently pushed him off. "Don't worry— I won't run off with it. I'll just carry it in for you. And as for the planes, as you see, they're not for us. Not for Weimar, either. Not today. Else by now we would be hearing . . ." He shook his head and did not finish the thought.

They had entered the building at last and were moving forward rapidly, along one side of a big room. Coming away from the head of the line with steaming mugs and chunks of dark bread in their hands, people were finding places at the long tables and benches that filled the room. Feeling calmer now, Stefan gazed about, on the lookout for a familiar face. Just one. Even Martin's.

Stefan turned to the man. "Were those American planes?" he asked.

"You don't know?"

"My dad and I only just arrived in Germany yesterday."

"Where from?" the man continued his questions.

"From Prague. But before that . . ."

Before that were the miles upon miles of sometimes headlong flight along with many thousands of others, German troops in rout and civilians alike, across Ukraine, through village after nameless village, town after town, the Red Army just at their backs driving them along like dry leaves in a hurricane.

Burdened with bundles of their worldly goods, men, women, and children had crowded the roads. All the world, it seemed, had left home and was on the move, struggling to escape at last the rule of terror under which they had lived ever since the seizure of their lands by the Soviets. Even cattle had been driven along, lowing continually in their primeval longing for rest, for lost stalls. Through snow and mud, under bombardment and strafing into Poland. Across Slovakia, into Czechia to Prague. And, at last, into the only remaining refuge, Germany itself.

Germany, their twin foe.

But that's where the Americans are headed. It stands to reason. Just look at the map! They and their Allies are already in Belgium and Holland. Germany next! And the quicker the better, for to the east the Soviets are already smashing their way toward Germany.

We'll meet with the Americans in Germany. And they will save us from both the Germans and the Russians. You can depend upon that. For they are a nation of freedom and they understand those who strive for it.

Stefan shook the jangle of remembered voices out of his head. He was standing at the head of the line by now, and the woman doling out the bread and soup was asking, "Well, where's your mug?"

"I . . . I forgot it."

The woman put her arms akimbo. "Forgot? Then out you go! No mug, no soup. That's the rule. Next!"

His ears burning, Stefan obediently began to turn away. But his new acquaintance caught him by the arm and stopped him. "Just a minute," he said to the woman in an affable tone. "You can give him a mug, can't you? Or at least the bread."

"And what else?" the woman cried, her voice rising. "The kid's sneaked in for a free handout, that's sure. Else he would have got a mug like everyone else registered here."

"No, listen, you don't understand. They only just arrived last night, he and his father and—"

Behind them, people began to grumble aloud. "Move on! We haven't got all day!"

Stefan tugged at the man's elbow. "It's all right," he whispered. "I'm not really hungry."

"Look, my good woman," the man persisted, "give the boy something to eat just this one time and if it turns out that he is indeed—heaven forbid—some sort of imposter, worming his way into our private club—"

"Move on! Move on up there!"

Stefan would have run off, but the man had hold of the valise.

"Well, all right. But I'm not supposed to let anyone through without a mug." And, grumbling to

26

herself, she handed Stefan a piece of bread and a steaming mug of some dark liquid with bits of what might be potato peelings visible in it.

When they had moved out of earshot, the man said, "You oughtn't to be so ready, my boy, to cave in before bureaucracy. Be a soldier against bureaucracy! That's my motto and I urge you to adopt it, too." He led the way to a table. "And why the devil do you lug this valise about with you? Eh?" he asked, as he set it down and took his place at the table. "What have you got in it that's so valuable?"

Before answering, Stefan took the opportunity to move the valise closer to his own legs. Then he sat down. "It's my father's," he said at last, avoiding the question.

That's daddy's valise and you mustn't play with it . . . else you'll break it.

That was his mother's voice a long time ago, when he was little. Just this once he allowed himself the sound of her voice.

But as for one of his own best possessions, that he had had to leave behind. "Just where do you think you're going? To a wedding?" his father had said when he proposed taking his accordion along on their flight before the onrushing Red Army.

"It'll be no trouble . . . I'll carry it myself on my back!"

"How far? No, Stefko. You're not quite a child any more, so you must understand. We must go as lightly as possible. For who knows how far we'll have

27

to travel?" Then his father, his voice turned gentle, had added, "Some day you will have another accordion. I can promise you that."

Only the week before their departure, they had buried Stefan's mother. She had died of pneumonia. It was then that Stefan's father had made the fateful decision. "We won't live another day under the Soviets," he said. "We'll go West, Stefko. West . . ."

All the same, leaving the accordion behind had been a wrench. At first, in the fever of leaving home before dawn on that day, their last in Poltava, he had scarcely felt the loss of his accordion. Running down the stairs of the apartment house, with a last glance backward, they had been off to join the growing column of refugees making their way westward out of Poltava. But later, every time Stefan thought of his accordion, like now, a sharp regret stabbed his inner flesh.

A neighbor had once remarked that the accordion was a common instrument of little musical value. "If you'd only spend as much time learning the violin, Stefko!"

"It doesn't matter," his father had countered. "He isn't in any case going to be a virtuoso. So let him pursue what he likes best."

Now Stefan was suddenly struck by his father's recollected remark, so at odds. Always at odds.

At the Palace of Pioneers to which he had belonged, he had been offered lessons on the accordion with the idea that, if he learned well, he could give

28

pleasure to others. His father, on the other hand, had approved his taking accordion lessons simply because he, Stefan, would find enjoyment in it.

And that was the very kind of thinking that, in the end, had done his father in, and had brought them, homeless, to this nation of strangers and enemies. Others' fathers had done what was expected of them, complied with rules both written and unwritten and . . .

Here Stefan's thoughts were routed by a single, overriding truth: even some of those who had ever so carefully, ever so abjectly complied had, in the end, been caught up and done away with. That's where the terror lay, that a person did not really know what was expected of him.

Stefan's gaze returned to the man beside him. "And who might your father be?" the man was asking.

"Wasylenko—Stefan, like me."

The man leaned backward in astonishment. "Would that be the botanist?"

Stefan smiled and nodded.

"Then I know your father by reputation! Imagine meeting him here! But then, there are millions of us here now, from every corner of the Soviet."

Without being asked, the man said that his own name was Behun and that he had been a professor of Latin in a secondary school in Drohobych in western Ukraine. But now he was teaching Latin to the refugee children.

Stefan sat and listened, wondering once again at

29

this talkativeness. At home in Poltava, he had never met with such voluble people as those he was meeting from western Ukraine.

Now the tone of the man's voice suddenly struck him. For all that he kept addressing him as "my boy," he was speaking to him as to another grown-up, instead of only to a half-grown boy. Usually, people took him to be younger than his fourteen years. As he chewed the bread and sipped the evil-tasting soup, he considered whether he liked the feeling of being taken for a grown-up. To his own surprise, he felt a certain distress—even panic—at the very thought. "Wait!" he wanted to shout. "Wait!"

Instead, he asked, "What does OST mean?"

"Ost? Why that's—you mean the armbands?"

Stefan nodded.

"They're the ones the Germans transported from all over the Soviet for forced labor here. They have to wear the armbands to show who they are. It means 'east.' " Mr. Behun looked at him, a curious amusement glinting in his eyes. "It means us."

"But then do we all have to wear one?"

"No, no, my boy. Not us. Only the young people who were caught in the net at home by the Germans and transported here."

In Poltava, that day, parents had come running out of their apartments to plead with the German SS men for their children. It had made no difference. In the end, the parents had stood on the street, huddled in a group, watching their children being led away, small bundles in hand, down the street, out of sight. . . .

Stefan remembered.

Only by sheer luck that day had he himself escaped the net. He and Pavlo. They had been on their way home from somewhere and had just rounded the corner, when they had caught sight of the milling crowd and the SS men midway down the block. They both had known that uniform from afar, even if they couldn't see the death's head and crossbones insignia on the peak of the caps. They had turned and run for their lives and had not ventured home again till nearly curfew.

"There are so many of us refugees in Germany by now," Mr. Behun was saying, "that they've had to open this camp to us, too, just to keep us out of their sight. So we're all of a heap together here, the forced laborers and us ordinary refugees. We're not going to run away," he added. "There's nowhere to run any more." He rose from his chair. "Well, my boy, now I'm on my way to the employment bureau here in camp. I haunt them every day. I look forward to meeting your father tonight!" And then he was off.

Returning to his bunk a little later, Stefan pulled the box of soap out of his pocket and secured it in his pack again.

Of course, any bar of soap was worth its weight in gold nowadays, but this was no ordinary bar. It was still in its original box, on which were printed the English words, "Rose Soap." The oblong box, printed

31

all over with tiny red roses intertwined with gilt ribbon, was somewhat rubbed and faded, and the lid was missing. But no matter. The soap was special.

His mother had acquired it somewhere long before Stefan was born. And even though, during the hard times after World War I, it could have been bartered for some very good meals, it had been kept unused, awaiting—as his mother had once explained —an even more evil day.

More evil days came. In plenty. But in the end she had lived through the worst of times—and had died —without bartering away the soap. And now here it was, in her son's pack. But he would never barter it. Never! He'd die first.

The soap, however, had not survived intact all these years. A large chip was missing from it. Stefan remembered the incident well, even though it had happened when he was hardly past four.

Finding the bar of soap in a drawer one day, and intrigued by its oval pinkness, he had taken a kitchen knife and had rammed it into the soap to find out what was inside. A large chip of it flew off and the point of the knife struck the palm of his hand. Blood. Alarm. Howls of pain.

His mother had come running. Fortunately, the wound was a superficial one. But as soon as his mother had bandaged it with a big impressive cloth, she had scolded him. "Leave knives alone!" she had cried.

"But you didn't tell me!" he had wailed.

"Must you always be told?"

But then she had drawn him close and, in a gentle

voice, had said something more, something that later seemed important, somehow. But he had long ago forgotten what it was and, search his memory how he would, he could never recall it. Though he knew that his mother had meant to comfort him, her words had only given him a feeling of anxiety. That much he remembered . . . but what had she said?

Well, all that was ancient history by now. "Plant a cross upon yesterday." That was a favorite saying of his father's.

Stefan climbed into his bunk and lay staring at the dirty gray mattress overhead. Gradually, he became aware of the barracks. Though apparently many people had gone to work, the barracks was alive with sound and activity. In some of the bunks, people were reading or mending things. In some, mothers were looking after their infants; in others, neighbors were chatting. Little children played on the floor in the aisles, or in their parents' bunks. Near the door, a woman leaning over a battered bucket was washing what looked like diapers. In the center of the room, both men and women stood about the iron stove, atop which several pots were simmering.

Out of nowhere, the thought of Pavlo came wandering into Stefan's head. His best friend, like one of his best possessions, left behind. Without even a good-by. There had been no time. Already units of the Red Army were infiltrating the eastern suburbs of Poltava, and if his father were caught. . . .

When all this was over, would he ever find Pavlo again? Pavlo! I'll be back!

Once, during the morning, the boy Martin came. Seeing Stefan, he said, "Come on out! Some of us are getting up a game of ball!"

No. He couldn't abandon Pavlo.

"Thanks," he said, smiling. "I can't right now. I have to stay here till my dad get back."

He was glad for the ready excuse.

three

WITH EYES OF BRILLIANT BLUE, GRANNY SOPHIA looked from Stefan to his father and back again. "Yes," she said, drawing out the word and smiling an all but toothless smile, "clearly father and son!"

Stefan gave his father an appraising glance. Some might consider him good-looking. True, the lines of bitterness about his mouth were by now ineradicably etched into the soft flesh at the corners of the lips. But it was a strong mouth. Firm. It was the eyes, however, that seized and held attention, despite their indeterminate color, for they looked straight at one.

That was the trouble: those eyes spoke too plainly of the thought within.

No. Though they resembled each other and bore the same name, only outwardly were they alike. Yet, alike or not alike, Stefan felt a vast relief to see his father returned from Weimar, safe at last. But the trip had been in vain; his father had failed to find private quarters in return for work. "The hostels are full, too," he said, "just as they were yesterday."

"Your son," Granny Sophia continued, "worried about you all the day long. Lay in his bunk and nothing and no one could budge him."

Chagrined that the old woman had given him away, Stefan quickly put in, "I was just—I thought you'd want me to watch the valise, Dad."

"Okh, that valise!" the old woman babbled on, raising her eyes to heaven. "He clung to that for dear life!"

At this point, fortunately, Mr. Behun appeared and introduced himself. "I've been hearing of you for years, sir," he said, addressing Stefan's father in the old-fashioned form one hardly ever heard at home, except in mockery or derision.

But his father, Stefan noticed, also called Mr. Behun "sir."

Evidently, news had already spread through the barracks that the arrivals of the night before were Stefan Wasylenko, the well-known botanist, and his son, for soon a number of people dropped by to make their acquaintance.

Among them, to Stefan's surprise, was a familiar face. It was that of a middle-aged woman with curly yellow hair whom Stefan recognized at once as the doctor who had expertly—though with a certain air of detachment—attended the wounded in a refugee column that had been strafed near Lwiw in Ukraine. It seemed so long ago. Though neither he nor his father had exchanged a dozen words with her, the moment they caught sight of each other they greeted one another like old friends.

"We crossed the river Zbruch together into western Ukraine," Stefan's father explained to those witnessing the glad reunion.

Watching his father, who was now sitting on the bunk between Mrs. Natalia and the doctor, Stefan sensed a change in him. He had noticed it before from time to time on their long journey westward. His father was more animated, more open, and a new courtliness in his manner seemed to increase as the evening wore on.

At home, he had not been like those people, mostly quite old, who clung to the old ways, to the outmoded courtliness and civility. Such people had been shoved aside as of no value, as superfluous human beings. They moved in an aura of a vague and perpetual bewilderment, as if they had lost their way. As indeed they had.

But here his father had slipped into the old ways with such ease that now he seemed almost a stranger. Stefan wondered and, as he wondered a queasy feeling of uncertainty formed in the pit of his stomach. He kept his eyes on the two women, as if one or the other of them held some sort of key to the subtle change in his father.

Dr. Olha, as people in the barracks addressed her, occupied a bunk on the other side of the room. Since her arrival, some weeks before, she had undertaken to look after the sick and the ailing in the camp, sharing this task with another refugee physician. "But it's not easy," she told them. "The Germans will provide nothing and for medicine I have only a little aspirin left. I cannot get a prescription filled because I have no license to practice in Germany." She shrugged her shoulders. "I do what I can."

"And that's a great deal, dear lady!" Mr. Behun cried.

Another to make his appearance that evening was a man who bunked near the door of the barracks whom everyone called Mr. Volodko. He was a historian by profession. "But at present," he explained, "I help Dr. Olha with the school we've organized here for the youngsters."

"Please tell us one of your jokes," Granny Sophia urged him. "We can use a bit of a laugh."

Mr. Volodko turned to Stefan's father. "I'm collecting jokes about Stalin and the Soviets . . . and also about Hitler and the Nazis," he explained. "It's a bit of social history. Now here's a new one I got just today from a Latvian, over in the other barracks."

When the laughter had died down, his joke reminded someone else of another, and that one of another. Attracted by the laughter, others joined them. Soon half a dozen or more were vying for the floor with another joke to tell.

All this while, Stefan, leaning against the tier of bunks, listened half in fear. Although, he had already noticed, the farther West they traveled, the bolder the talk, it was best to be cautious even here.

Even if you've nothing to hide, don't blab all that

you're thinking. Rule number one. Stefan grinned inwardly. Rather, rules number one through ten!

Weren't any of these grown-ups aware of the dangers? Even at this distance? Why, for all that they knew he—or someone—was tucking away in his memory what was being said, and by whom and who had answered what, in order to carry it all later to interested authorities. For a reward, certainly, if only the reward of not being caught. That's the way it had been everywhere at home, and there was no reason to believe that the net of spying did not exist in Germany as well, even among the refugees from that same net. Yet here they were, on the surface sensible, sober adults, blabbing their heads off, talking all sorts of treason.

Stefan tried not to laugh at the jokes, but he couldn't help himself. Each was funnier than the last. After joining in the laughter, he gazed narrowly around from one to another of the group. Which one might be the spy? Mr. Behun? Mrs. Natalia, sitting there beside his father? For it was always the seemingly candid, friendly types. . . .

Someone poked him in the ribs and he started, as if out of a trance. "What are you thinking, with that funny look on your face?" Martin asked.

Stefan laughed. "Nothing," he said.

At last, to Stefan's relief, the jokes ceased. Granny Sophia began talking about herself. "We took refuge across the river that day," she said, looking around at them.

"Which river is that, Granny?" Stefan's father asked.

The old woman looked at him in surprise. "Why, our Dnipro!" she cried. "Our village was under fire from the Soviets—impossible for even a fly to find cover. So we threw some things into a bundle and all ran to the river and took to the boats. 'We'll come back,' we said, 'when the battle's over.'"

The old woman, her eyes suddenly watering, paused. "But somehow," she went on, in a moment, "the battle did not come to an end. Not that day nor the next, nor even the next. And our son was there, somewhere, in the Red Army. But who knows where? Then someone brought us the news that a shell had destroyed our hut."

"A Bolshevik shell?" Mr. Behun asked.

"What does it matter?" the old woman suddenly flared. "Bolshevik or Nazi, we people suffer. Sooner choose between Satan and Beelzebub. We suffer at the hands of both. God put us on this earth to enjoy life, to enjoy the beauty of His bright earth, yet there are people for whom this is not enough. So they must needs order everyone about, spoiling people's lives, perfect strangers to them—must needs go tramping and marching about the world. And to what purpose? Does it make them the happier?"

There was a long silence. Then the old woman sighed and resumed her story. "So we went on, and on, village to village, and the front always right at our backs."

"Your husband and you?" Dr. Olha asked.

"My old man. And then, in that village—Lord, when I think—we only stopped there by chance, to

40

spend the night. But some Red partisans fell upon two German soldiers in the village and killed them. And before that night was done, the Germans came and rounded up all of our men—boys among them, too—and to the market square with them. We begged and we pleaded, we women. We wept and we screamed. But, all the same, they hanged them . . . the boys, too."

"And there you have it," Mr. Volodko broke the silence that followed. "With German hands the Soviets murder our people. For, otherwise, what was the purpose of killing a couple of Germans?"

The old woman began to rock back and forth, keening in a high, piercing voice. "Okh, merciful God, receive their souls! Okh, God in heaven. . . ."

His gaze riveted upon the old woman's face, Stefan had stood listening to her every word. For all that, hers was hardly an unusual story. But when she uttered those quaint words, "Merciful God, receive their souls," it sounded odd to his ear. At home in Poltava such a phrase, if uttered at all, would have been spoken in jest, or in mockery. She, however, had used it seriously. But then, she was a peasant woman and peasants, Stefan assured himself, were always backward types.

"That would be perhaps in Volynia somewhere?" his father's words interrupted the woman's lament.

The old woman, recovering herself at last, nodded. "In Volynia province. But at least he lies in his native soil and among his own," she said, a defiant tone suddenly in her voice, as if for the hundredth time justifying the matter to herself. "And I wanted to return home, then and there. But there was no way to get back through the front. So I journeyed on . . . and here I am in a stranger's land. But among my own for all that." And her face lit with a faint smile at last.

Somehow, then, and as if from habit, the talk turned to the theme of "when the Americans come." When the Americans come, they will liberate us from our enemies, the Soviets and Nazis alike, rescue us from this miserable, homeless life.

Stefan stood listening to this talk, then turned and leaned down toward his father. "Dad," he whispered. "We will go home, won't we, Dad? When it's all over?"

His father only shrugged his shoulders. "Who knows, Stefko, what will happen? It all depends."

"But Dad, we have to!"

Otherwise they would never know at home what happened to him. Pavlo wouldn't know. His best friend, one with whom he had shared secrets the most secret, would, in the end, not know.

At home, after all this was over, Pavlo and the others would meet and talk things over among themselves. And, eventually, someone would say, "But I wonder whatever happened to Stefan Wasylenko?" And not one of them would know.

As for himself, he would have no one with whom to remember. But no . . . there might be a way. Some day he would grow up—and grown-ups did as they pleased, didn't they? So then he could go home, no matter what his father did.

". . . give the government what for," Mr. Behun was saying, evidently still talking about Americans and America.

Stefan grinned. Giving the authorities "what for" was such an unheard of, utterly absurd and bizarre idea that it was actually ludicrous—if not lunatic.

There was an old woman who had frequented the park near their flat in Poltava. She used to go shuffling along talking aloud to no one. "Antichrists! The whole lot of them! May they burn in hell. Them and their party!" And then she would spit in a sign of contempt.

The first time he had come upon her, he had run off as fast as his legs could carry him to get as far away as possible before the militia came. Later he told Pavlo about it, but cautiously had refrained from repeating the treasonous words.

Pavlo had interrupted him. "Haven't you ever seen her before?" He tapped his temple. "And so no one pays her attention."

Aside from that old woman he could not remember, ever in his life, having heard of a person giving the authorities "what for." Not in public. And in private . . . well, even there, best to be cautious.

What sort of land was that America, anyway, if the government allowed such things? Truly, the world was unhinged.

Yet, for the first time since they had left home, many months before, they were not on the run. That night when Stefan crawled into his bunk to sleep at last, he noticed that someone had pulled the black curtain over the window again, and it gave him a rare feeling of comfort. Just on the other side of that curtain, all was cold and darkness, danger and hostility. But here within, where he lay, was warmth and safety from both Nature and man. It was a place of refuge within the very heart of chaos.

four

THE NEXT MORNING, MR. BEHUN CAME BOUNDING
up as Stefan and his father sat eating with Martin
and his mother. "Good news, good people!" he cried.
"I've just learned at the employment bureau that
they're looking for qualified people for a special task.
Two or three who know various languages to help in
a library."

"Scholarly work!"

"But what languages?"

"The Slavic ones and Italian, French, Latin . . .
whatever. So I told them, 'We are of many professions in the camp. I believe I can even find you an
experienced librarian!' " He smiled at Mrs. Natalia.
"So come, my friends! Hurry to the bureau before
the word spreads."

"Books," Mrs. Natalia murmured, rising quickly.
"How good it would be to work with books again."

With that, the grown-ups hurried off, leaving Stefan and Martin to themselves. Soon they returned with the news that they had got the job and were to begin that very morning. The work was right in the nearby village, and they were to get not only cash pay but one meal a day as well. "And don't forget the cigarettes, once a week or so!" Mr. Behun said.

Cigarettes!

"Probably only the Sport brand," Stefan's father remarked.

"All the same," Mr. Behun countered, "by now even Germans are glad to take the Sport brand in trade."

"Dad, I'm glad we're going to stay!" Stefan cried, overcome by the sudden good luck.

"With the bedbugs?" His father gave him an amused look.

"I don't care!" Stefan cried, passionately. "I just want to stay in one place!"

"I hope not for long," his father replied, "because, eventually, we must find something better."

That morning, before setting off for work, his father made arrangements for Stefan to join the daily classes organized and taught by the refugees themselves. From first-graders to secondary-school pupils like Martin, there were only about twenty in the whole "school." But Dr. Olha and Mr. Volodko, who were in charge, strove to teach a variety of subjects—whatever they had pupils for—math, reading, writing, history, geography, and, at Dr. Olha's insistence, hygiene.

"At night," Martin explained to Stefan, as they sat waiting in the mess hall for school to begin, "I'm studying Latin with Mr. Behun. He's teaching Ukrainian and German, too."

To Stefan it felt good to be back in school, even this makeshift one, after more than a year's absence. But though Dr. Olha and Mr. Volodko both proved to be strict teachers, he was mildly shocked at what seemed to him misconduct on the part of some of the pupils. Two of the girls, for example, kept whispering to each other the whole time. And some of the pupils, including Martin and a broad-shouldered, blond-headed boy named Olexa, were continually jumping up and asking questions. It hadn't been that way at home! Stefan wasn't at all sure that he liked the difference.

After school that day, Stefan joined Martin and some of the other boys in a game of soccer. Well, they called it soccer, but the ball was only a rubber beach ball that belonged to one of the Latvian boys—wherever he had got it. Unfortunately, it had developed a leak, so that at the end of every single game they had to blow it up again.

Across the narrow road from the yard was a prisoner-of-war camp. Judging by the obviously wasted condition of the prisoners, they must have been Red Army men. "The Germans wouldn't dare treat Americans that way," Martin said.

Standing well back from the barbed wire, the prisoners watched the soccer games from afar, their wizened faces split by grins.

Of the eight boys playing, only Stefan, Martin, and Olexa were Ukrainian. But everybody spoke a motley jargon, made up of all the languages of eastern Europe, plus a goodly dash of German.

Late in the afternoon, the game broke up. Hungry as a wolf, Stefan followed Martin back into the barracks. Fortunately, he had saved a piece of bread from that morning; so, as soon as he reached his bunk, he ferreted it out and ate it to the very last crumb. Then he settled back, arms under head, to await his father's return from his first day at work. And for the second time in two days he felt that same rare contentment.

The winter dusk had already fallen before the grown-ups returned. Stefan's father was the first to make his appearance. One look at him and Stefan could not believe his eyes. His father's face and hands were streaked with dirt but, worst of all, the front of his coat, which he had shaken out and brushed so carefully before starting out that morning, was black with grime. Mrs. Natalia presented nearly the same appearance. So did Mr. Behun.

"Mercy upon us!" Granny Sophia exclaimed. "What in heaven's name has befallen you three?"

Stefan's father gave a short laugh. "We've been doing scholarly work!"

"But Dad! What happened?"

His father struggled out of his coat and tossed it into his bunk. By now, a little group had gathered, Dr. Olha and Mr. Volodko among them, gazing in wonder at the "scholarly" workers. The three of them took turns describing their day. It turned out that the

48

men's work consisted of unloading loose books out of a boxcar standing on a spur of the railroad that skirted the village, and transporting them in wheelbarrows to a large stone building in the courtyard of an old castle perched upon a hilltop near the center of the village.

There Mrs. Natalia sorted the books by category and language and placed them on shelves. "And those books," she said, "seem to have been on the road even longer than we have! Just look at my hands!"

"But where did they come from?" Stefan asked.

"Why, from all the great libraries of Europe!" Mr. Behun declared.

"Kiev, too?" Mr. Volodko asked. "Not Kiev?"

"Kiev, too. And Lwiw. And Poltava. And Kharkiw. And Krakow. And Vienna. And Paris. And Brussels. And—"

"Stolen?"

"You might say stolen. Yes, you might put it that way," Mrs. Natalia said.

This ironical turn of events so tickled the fancy of the grown-ups that they spent that evening telling anecdotes of similar farcical tricks that fortune had played on them in the past. That night everyone went to bed lighthearted, refreshed by laughter.

Every day, while his father was at work, Stefan met new boys and girls, for every day more people appeared in the camp, seeking shelter from the world. But making friends was scarcely worth-while, for some soon left and others took their places. "We're tired of spending most of our time killing bedbugs," those

49

leaving said. "We can starve elsewhere in greater comfort."

Nearly every day, too, planes appeared in the sky overhead. Flying Fortresses. But they passed on. To Dresden, some said. To Berlin. To Hamburg.

In general, however, except for talk of "when the Americans come," the war was scarcely ever discussed in the barracks. No one ever saw a newspaper and rarely did anyone hear a radio. And when they did, the war reports only brought derisive snorts from the grown-ups. They'd all heard the same song before, when the Red Army was in full rout before the German onslaught, four years before. Then one only heard: "After defeating the invader in a decisive battle, the victorious units of the glorious Red Army have moved to previously prepared positions."

They had been there and knew that "moving to previously prepared positions" simply meant, first, disposing of all the political prisoners in the prisons; then taking off in a chaos of headlong flight, dropping weapons and abandoning burned-out tanks and stalled trucks all the long way clear to Stalingrad. And here in Germany it was the same: the Wehrmacht was retreating from victory to victory.

Among the grown-ups, not the war but food and ration cards, passports, passes, and bedbugs were the chief topics of conversation. Some people, it was whispered, were even finding lice. And more and more often now they came upon what looked to the eye and felt upon the tongue suspiciously like chaff in the bread which they got with their ration cards.

50

Whether this was a sign of the coming defeat or merely the universal chronic shortage of springtime they could not agree. Whichever it was, hunger gnawed at them all more sharply than ever.

As for Stefan and his new friends, they too talked about food much of the time. But sometimes they talked about themselves.

One day, Martin announced that he had an uncle in America.

America!

Martin nodded, that self-possessed look on his face. "Sure. He went over before the war. He's married and has children. So now I have American cousins, too."

Stefan was stunned. American cousins! "What— what does your uncle do there in America?" he managed to ask.

"Well, he had a hard time. He was trained to be a lawyer, see, but in America all he could get was a factory job. And he was lucky to get that. But my cousins—one of them is a doctor and the other a school teacher—they put themselves through school."

"But didn't the government register him as a lawyer and assign him a job?"

"The government? What do you mean, the government? The government doesn't assign in America. You're on your own. In America, you're on your own, brother!"

Afterward, Stefan tried to imagine what it would be like to be on his own, completely on his own, and in a strange land. But all he succeeded in doing was to generate a feeling of panic within himself. He could not imagine deliberately going to a land like that. How did people there manage, if everything depended upon themselves? For a long time he pondered this question, but found no answer.

Though Stefan was hungry most of the time, and though the discomforts of the barracks were many, he had begun to forget some of the terrors of the road. He felt as if, after hanging onto a bear's tail and not daring to let go, now of a sudden, in this unlikely haven, he could safely do so. The world could rage and storm all around him and he could dwell in the calm eye without concern.

The return to some of the routines of home helped. Every morning his father and the other grown-ups went to work while Stefan and the other pupils went to "school." Just like home, Dr. Olha, Mr. Volodko, and Mr. Behun gave them homework to do. At home, it had often been annoying when one or the other of his parents interrupted some pleasant pastime of his with the command, "To your books!"

Usually, this had been his mother, since his father had so often been absent on his job. But in either case it had been irksome. Now here in this refuge, this place of exile, Stefan felt an odd comfort when his father, once more after such a long interruption, began to say in the evening, "To your books!"

Of course, the phrase was only a manner of speaking, because in fact they had no schoolbooks among them. For that matter, it was not easy even to find paper and pencil with which to work his math problems. Every scrap of paper that came their way was saved for writing on, over and over.

Day after day now drifted by so unremarkably that Stefan all but forgot about his father's valise that, until recently, had loomed so large in his mind. It had been stowed under the tier of bunks. Out of sight, out of mind.

One evening, however, his father suddenly brought it forth from its hiding place. It happened that Granny Sophia had been recalling certain herbs from home and what remedies they were good for. When she began to describe a certain plant, and Mrs. Natalia remarked that she had never seen it, Stefan's father roused. "Ah, I know that plant!" he exclaimed. "Wait, I'll show you!"

And with that he got out of his bunk and dragged his valise from underneath it. Heaving it up onto his bunk, he began to undo the rope tied around it. From across the aisle Granny Sophia and the others watched with interest.

"You mean to say, sir," Granny Sophia burst out at last, "that you have been lugging about with you a suitcase filled with dead plants—weeds—under fire and in flight? My dear sir! Excuse me, but to what purpose?"

Stefan grinned appreciatively. But in the next instant, when he saw the others smiling, too, unexpectedly he felt himself bristling. What right had they to make light of his father's work?

"No," his father answered quietly. "Not the plants themselves, Granny, but drawings of them—hundreds.

And a manuscript, all but finished—a large work on the plants of Ukraine."

"So your valise is full of drawings and papers?" The old woman laughed. "And I thought—we thought that it surely must be filled with treasure!"

Mrs. Natalia suddenly spoke. "There's treasure . . . and treasure, Granny," she said softly, her eyes alight.

"This valise," Stefan's father went on, opening it at last, "contains my life's work." He straightened and looked at Mrs. Natalia. "My legacy to the world."

Stefan stared up at his father. He had never heard him speak so solemnly of his work. But then he remembered how, whenever his father had been home with them, he used to work long hours over the drawings and the manuscript. It had not been part of his job, but a task he had set for himself.

Stefan, young though he was at the time, had sensed that there was something forbidden and therefore dangerous in this work of his father's. Once, he had overheard his mother whisper, fearfully, "Oh, be careful, my darling. What if they should find out?"

And his father had replied, "As much as we can, my dear, let us live free."

In the end, he was indeed found out. Their apartment had been burst into by the secret police and searched. His father had been arrested for something called "bourgeois nationalist activity." That was a crime worse than murder. And "nationalists" were arch "enemies of the people."

Fortunately, the secret police had found and confiscated only one of two copies of the manuscript and merely a handful of drawings. The rest had been placed in hiding in a friend's apartment.

Granny Sophia and the others were gazing at the drawings one by one. Admiration shone on every face.

"Exquisite. . . ." Mrs. Natalia murmured.

five

LIKE BIRDS OF PASSAGE, BATTERED BY WIND AND
storm, people continued to pass through the camp.
Some, like Stefan and his father, chose to stay for a
time. Others soon left. Still others, refugees like themselves, came for just the day, to give lectures, attend
meetings, or just to visit friends. The lectures were on
a wide variety of unlikely topics—whatever the speaker
was versed in. Unlikely or not, however, these events
were always attended by nearly everyone in the camp.

One never-to-be-forgotten Saturday, a troupe of
singers and dancers arrived. They, however, were not
refugees but artists detained by the Gestapo, the
German secret police. Virtual captives, they had been
shipped from Kiev to Hamburg, Germany. There
they were forced to work long and exhausting hours
in a factory. In time, however, they managed to talk
their captors into allowing them to return to their

real work and even to go on a tour of the work and refugee camps and hostels.

Everyone in the entire camp, from infant to grandparent, attended the performance that night, packing the mess hall to the walls. Some people wept to hear once more, in this harsh and alien place, the songs of home. Though it was a bitter cold night, the windows and doors were kept open so that the prisoners of war in the camp across the road might share in the occasion.

The audience would not let the artists go, and despite their weariness and their obvious emaciation, they sang and danced till nearly midnight. Afterward, moving with the crowd out into the starry night, Stefan thought he caught a special look on his father's face as he leaned toward Martin's mother and said something to her. But to Stefan's relief she did not return the look. Instead, she called attention to the silent faces, gaunt and white in the bright moonlight, that clustered at the windows of the POW barracks across the road.

Stefan was spending nearly ever waking hour with Martin now, attending classes with him, doing homework with him sometimes, playing ball with him nearly every day. Several afternoons a week, he and Martin and Olexa accompanied a couple of the men into the great surrounding forest to gather firewood for the barracks stove. They had permission from the camp authorities to chop up fallen logs for their use. From somewhere they had acquired a child's battered old sled and they used this to haul out the wood.

Stefan had never been in such dense forest before. The deep winter silence, the dark green—almost black —of the pines and firs, the all but concealed hiding places that he glimpsed fleetingly, out of which secret eyes must surely be watching as they made their way along—all set his heart to pounding with a not unpleasant primeval fear. He would never venture into such a place alone, he told himself.

A faint odor of fungus always hovered on the air.

They used to spend the day in the woods, gathering mushrooms, he and his parents, all three. At noon, when he had grown ravenous, his mother would spread a cloth under a tree and lay out the lunch she had packed. They'd eat and his parents would talk. Those were the only times he could remember of being together as a family, those rare, brief times when his father had been at home with them, on leave from whatever village he had been currently assigned to.

His father had taught him to recognize several varieties of mushrooms that were edible. And it was he, Stefan, who, the summer he was six, made the best find of any of them, ever. He never thought of himself as a lucky person, but this find was a stroke of rare good luck.

There it waited under the pine tree just for him and no one else—a huge cauliflower mushroom, not less than a third of a meter across. It was so huge that he could not lift it out of the ground by himself without breaking it. So he had called to his parents. After appropriately marveling at his find, together they had carefully loosened the mushroom from its mooring and wrapped it in the lunch cloth.

On the tramway home that day, his father had bid him to unwrap the cloth and display his find to those around them. News of it had traveled up and down the car and he was repeatedly pointed out as its discoverer.

Best of all, as soon as they had reached the city, his father had hunted for one of the itinerant photographers that plied their trade—illegal because it was private—at the center of town, around the big Monument to Glory. There he had had his picture taken, all by himself, standing triumphant beside the monument, that served as a prop for his monster mushroom. Then, for good measure, they all had their picture taken grouped around it.

And where were those pictures now? In one of them his mother had stood smiling beside him, her hand resting lightly on his shoulder. He remembered that.

Even a year later, they were still eating that mushroom, for his mother had cut it up into small pieces to dry. He remembered. He had cried bitterly when, one morning, he came upon her cutting up his mushroom. He wanted to keep it forever.

"I want to keep it!" he had blubbered. "It's mine!"

Now, trudging through this German forest with Martin and Olexa, he remembered his mother's reply. "But Stefko, it won't keep! Nothing ever stays the same!"

One day, as Stefan and the other two boys trekked homeward from the forest, taking turns at pulling the loaded sled, Martin, who had been in the camp longer than Stefan or Olexa, told them something about the forest. Within it, he informed them, somewhere between the village and Weimar to the south, were some sort of military installations.

"And there's a concentration camp in this forest, too," Olexa broke in, "called Buchenwald."

Stefan caught his breath. "How do you know?" he asked, his voice suddenly lowered to a whisper.

"Because one of my uncles is an inmate there, we found out. My dad went there to find out about him. It's his brother, see."

They fell into a frightened silence. Then Martin whispered, "I wouldn't go there."

"Me, neither," Stefan echoed. "Not for anything!"

"You would if it was your brother," Olexa said.

"Oh, in that case. . . ." Martin murmured.

But Stefan only pursed his lips in doubt.

Olexa suddenly broke the silence. "My big brother was burned."

"Burned?" Martin asked. "How do you mean 'burned'?"

"I mean burned," Olexa repeated. "The Soviets arrested him and all the other students in his school and put them in prison. And then, when they started their retreat, they burned down the prison."

"With them still inside?"

"Inside."

Later, one day, when the three of them were alone

again, Martin broke off a series of questions he was asking Stefan about his life at home and, in exasperation cried, "I can't make you out, Stefko! You're the most closemouthed fellow I've ever met!"

"You said it!" Olexa agreed, laughing.

"I am?"

"Yes, you are. We tell you things. But you never tell us anything."

Stefan smiled. "Because there's nothing much to tell," he lied.

There's too much. That's the trouble. Too much. And besides, best to take care. Best not to make fast friends, then risk another good-by. He had had enough of good-bys to last him a lifetime.

But Martin persisted. "So what about your mother?" he asked. "You never speak of her."

"She's dead."

"Oh! Then . . ."

"My dad," Stefan quickly began, to forestall any further questions about his mother, "was in prison for 'nationalist activity.' But he was lucky. When the war began they let him out of prison—but he had to join a penal squad right away."

"What's that?" Olexa asked.

"That's . . . well, the squad had to go across mine fields . . . to set off any mines."

"German mines?" Olexa asked.

"Well, sometimes Russian ones, too," Stefan replied. "And the squad always had to go first at the beginning of an attack. So as to draw the German fire away from the Red Army troops, see? They weren't

61

allowed to carry any weapons, so my dad was the only one that survived. But they kept putting him into new squads."

"So then did he escape . . . or what?" Martin asked.

"He had a friend in the regular troops and this friend helped him escape. So then he came back to Poltava."

Martin seemed satisfied by this revelation, for the time.

And then, among all the ordinary days, came that one memorable one, one that afterward lingered on and on in Stefan's thoughts. It was the day that he went with Martin to the nearby village for the first time.

When they reached it, they followed its narrow, cobbled main street as it wound its way toward the market square. The street was littered with horse manure, wisps of hay, and other debris. On either side, along the very edge of the street, two-story buildings with steeply gabled roofs stood in tight rows, no spaces between. Though the houses looked ancient, they stood as if newly washed. And high over the little village, as if to complete the scene, on its own little hill towered the old castle where the grown-ups were at work.

"It's a medieval village," Martin informed him. "I've seen pictures."

Stefan gazed in wonder as they walked along. Not a heap of rubble anywhere, not a chimney standing lone, not a broken, blackened wall. . . . The whole village intact. The landscape undisfigured by even so much as a tank or truck standing burned and abandoned beside the road. And how still it was! No music of distant cannon, no roaring of planes overhead . . . no corpses. And over there, on that well-scrubbed doorstep, a miracle: a cat dozing in the winter sun.

So this is what it is like. . . .

Stefan stared at the windows as they passed. Over some of them hung light filmy curtains. But mostly they looked blank, like a blind person's eyes as, heedless of the two boys, they stared sightless at the windows opposite. All the same, each of those windows meant home to someone. That was the main thing. To be home. Somewhere.

The people they met stared at them as they walked along. But Stefan, fortified by the companion at his side, did not mind as much as if he had been alone. Some cast them unfriendly glances. But a few nodded and one even gave them something of a smile.

At last they reached the little market square. It was empty today, but its four sides were lined with shops. There was a cobbler's shop, then a tiny restaurant, and next to that a pastry shop.

Here they stopped and wordlessly gazed into its window. Fortunately for their better sanity, the display of pastries in the window was fake: small buns and rolls, cookies and fancy pastries, obviously made of some sort of paste, highly colored to simulate browned butter, glazed sugar, chocolate—oh, chocolate!—and bright red cherries.

After a long while, they moved on. When they came

to a meat shop, they stopped again. A row of sausages was strung along the back of its window. "Like a bead curtain," Stefan said, reminded of one that Pavlo's mother had at home.

"Like a bead curtain made of sausages," Martin amended.

"That's the best kind!" Stefan cried.

They burst into hilarious laughter. At this, the proprietor, a plump woman, came out waving her fat bleached arms at them. "Raus! Raus!" she shouted.

Martin couldn't stop laughing. "We're rausing," he said, making a Ukrainian word of the German.

They turned, and there stood a policeman. As usual, Stefan at once felt himself stiffen inside. Planting himself in front of them, a severe look on his face, the policeman said, "Documents."

Of course, documents. The word was the same in Ukrainian. An international word. Documents everywhere. For if you had no papers, who were you? Nobody. Papers were as vital to life as food and air, perhaps even more so.

He dug into his jacket pocket and brought forth his pass, issued by the Gestapo, permitting him to travel into Germany. Martin did the same. Scarcely glancing at the documents, the policeman handed them back. Then, giving them a final sharp look, he strode on.

Subdued now, by silent consent the two boys made their way back across the square and started for home, choosing a street at random. Now and again, they came to a casement window standing slightly ajar.

Through them came snatches of talk and even the intimate clink of china.

Stefan couldn't bear it. "Come on!" he said, breaking into a run. But he had gone only a few steps when he heard a sound that halted him in his tracks.

Music!

He looked up. It was coming through an open window on the second level. An accordion. . . . Someone was playing an accordion! And expertly, too.

Martin, standing beside him, tugged at his sleeve. "Come on," he urged.

No, wait. . . .

There was something joyous in that sound! As soon as one heard it, visions of weddings, dances, merry occasions of every sort came alive in the mind's eye. . . .

He recalled his father's words: "Some day you will have another accordion. I can promise you that."

But would he? Ever again?

"Are you coming?" Martin asked.

Yes . . . coming.

That night, remembrance of the accordion he had heard would not let him fall asleep. He tossed and he turned as wild, impossible thoughts crowded into his head. What if he should go back to that house, boldly knock on the door, and ask to see the accordion player? What if they should let him in? What if the accordion player said, "Sure. Here. Try it"? What if, after hearing him play, he said, "Come back again! Any time!"

six

STEFAN AWOKE THE NEXT MORNING WITH THE DETERMINATION to go back to the house of the accordion that very day. It was a Sunday, so he was free of classes. Remembering Martin's impatience of the day before, he decided to go alone this time. Then, if the improbable happened and his dream of actually playing the instrument came true, maybe he could bring Martin the next time. Olexa, too.

But it wasn't easy to get away from Martin. Despite the rather elaborate casualness with which Stefan made his way toward the door of the barracks that morning, Martin called after him, "Hey, Stefko, wait for me!"

Stefan turned. "I'll be outside," he said, and continued on his way.

Once safely out of the barracks, he made a run for the gate and did not slacken his pace until he had gone well past it. It was a sunny morning, not too cold. And that was especially good, Stefan thought to himself, because then the window of the house of the accordion would more likely be open again.

Just as he reached the village, a church bell began ringing, and he saw people ahead of him walking toward the market square where the church stood. Following along behind them, he came to the street he was looking for and soon found the house. But, to his disappointment, all the windows were closed.

He stood across the narrow street and stared at the upper window from which the music had come. He strained his eyes for a glimpse of what might be inside. But he could see nothing and no one appeared at the window.

For a long while, unmindful of the passersby brushing past him, Stefan stood staring up at the window, trying to will it open. Perhaps if someone inside saw him, he might open the window and ask what he wanted. At long last, however, he turned away. He'd take a little walk and come back again. After all, it was still early. Probably the accordion player was still sound asleep. Or perhaps he had gone to church.

Stefan was sorry now that he hadn't stopped for breakfast that morning for he was dying of hunger as he walked along. If only he had stowed a little something in his pocket!

After a while, impatient of putting it off any longer, he turned back and retraced his steps. But when he reached the house again, he found the window as tightly shut as ever.

Now he began to eye the door. What would happen if he simply knocked on it, just as he had dreamed of doing? But though he could dream boldly enough, the doing was another matter altogether.

It was turning colder and, now and again, he had to stamp his feet and beat his arms to get warm. And then it happened. While he stood there trying to pluck up enough courage to step up to the door, he heard a grating sound.

With a glad smile on his face, Stefan looked up. The window opened and a woman's head appeared over the sill. She looked down at him, anger on her face. "What are you hanging about for?" she shouted down at him. "I'll call the police!"

Stefan stood for an instant, speechless, unable to believe his ears. Then he turned and, without once looking back, ran as if devils were chasing him.

He slowed only when he came within sight of the barracks. The boys, he saw, were out in the yard playing soccer, Martin among them. It occurred to him that he had never once mentioned to Martin anything at all about the accordion he had once had but had had to leave behind. So how could Martin have understood how important it was? Perhaps if he had had Martin along with him this morning, instead of going off on his own, things might have turned out differently.

As he came in through the gate, Martin spied him. "Hey, come on, Stefko!" he yelled. "We've been waiting for you! Where were you?"

"In a minute!" Stefan called. "I have to go in for a second."

He wanted to get the piece of bread he had stored in his bunk. Then he'd be ready to play soccer all the rest of the morning. Once inside, he hurried down the aisle toward his bunk. But when he came within sight of it, he halted.

His father and Mrs. Natalia were sitting on the edge of his bunk, alone. His father's hands cupped hers and, as they gazed at each other, he seemed to be murmuring something to her. Mrs. Natalia's eyes, more luminous than ever, shone large and deep and dark. Neither seemed aware of Stefan.

For a long moment, he stood and stared. Then, he turned on his heel and ran blindly out of the barracks, his head suddenly bursting. He stumbled to the place behind the mess hall, where the firewood was stacked, and sat down on a log.

In the old days he sometimes used to come upon his parents sitting by themselves that very same way, oblivious of his presence, and murmuring something to each other. And now, in place of his mother, this woman, this stranger. . . .

Plant a cross upon yesterday. Of course. And plant a cross upon his mother. She was dead.

No. She was not dead. She had not died. That was only . . . she could not be dead. How could his father believe that? How could he imagine that anyone else could ever take her place? Stefan had not relinquished her. How could his father?

And yet, the memory of her was fading. Already, he thought sadly, he could not picture her in his mind's eye without great effort. Her image simply refused to appear. That disturbed him profoundly, as if something of great price had been slipping away and he had been wholly unaware of it. Nor could he any longer easily remember anything she had ever said or had ever done. Too much had happened. Too much. . . .

He had a sudden curious thought. It was as if she herself had the power of receding into the past and was doing it deliberately. Purposely. But no, his mother would never abandon him. He had to brush that terrible thought aside.

From around the corner of the mess hall, Martin appeared. "Hey, what are you doing here, Stefko? We're waiting for you." He came up and seized him by the shoulder. "Stefko?"

Stefan suddenly thrust out an arm and gave him a shove. "You leave me alone, you hear? Just leave me alone!" he shouted, as Martin staggered backward and fell with a thud.

seven

AFTER THAT DAY STEFAN WAS NOT ABLE TO LOOK HIS father in the eye, as if something shameful lay between them. Yet his father seemed quite unaware of it. That was another point against him, Stefan told himself.

He watched his father and Mrs. Natalia like a hawk, on the alert for further signs of some understanding between them. And since he searched, he found.

It seemed to him that whenever Mrs. Natalia's eyes rested upon his father, they grew more luminous than ever. And deeper. And his father's the same. For the first time, he saw painful significance in the fact that they were often to be found side by side.

Granny Sophia noticed, too. Trust her! One day, she made some remark about "you two"—meaning Mrs. Natalia and his father—as if acknowledging some bond between them. One thing, however, heartened

Stephan enormously: "those two" were still address-ing one another in the formal plural form.

Stefan longed to talk over his fears with someone and he counted over one by one who that someone might be. Certainly not Martin! No, and not Olexa, either. He sighed. It could only be Pavlo. And Pavlo was no longer of his world. There was no one.

Unless . . . his father? Why not his father? Con-front him! Remind him. Remind him that his son had by no means forgotten his mother, as he him-self apparently had. In his thoughts, Stefan spoke his feelings in bitter words to match the bitterness within himself. But as for actually making the oc-casion and uttering the words—that he could not bring himself to do.

However, he did manage to keep his distance from Martin. That much he could do. Perhaps if it were noticed that he and Martin were not at all good friends, their parents would have second thoughts. Several times he caught Martin eyeing him, a puzzled expression in his eyes.

"Just leave me alone," Stefan muttered to himself, turning away.

And then, one day, to Stefan's great embarrassment, as if he had been found out in something wrong, his father himself spoke to him, not in direct words, but plainly enough.

"You know, Stefko," he began, "when all this is over that we are living through, we must begin again. We will settle somewhere—in the West, since it has come to that. And I will find work. We must form a family again. But you and I don't make a family. Do you understand?"

Stefan looked away, anger and grief choking him to suffocation.

"We cannot ever return to the old days," his father continued. "That's gone. The important thing is to begin again. Your mother would want it so."

That episode only threw Stefan into further despair. He did not know what to do or how to behave. But that very same day, a Sunday, other events thrust all this aside.

On that Sunday afternoon, the Flying Fortresses came flying over, as they did nearly every day now. As usual, anxious faces turned heavenward. Not on us, please God! Not on us. And, as usual, the planes flew on.

But only moments after the planes had passed overhead, from the direction of Weimar came a sound that brought everyone bolting out of the barracks. Bukh-Bukh-Bukh-Bukh! Four times in rapid succession, then a slight pause, and another cluster of four.

While people stared, transfixed, the gray sky over Weimar began to redden. Like blood on the water of a pond the red oozed across the leaden sky. As squadron after squadron roared by overhead, the explosions suddenly seemed even closer, shaking the very ground beneath their feet.

"Look! That's the forest they're bombing!"

"Okh, yes! The munitions dump!"

"Run!"

"Where? There's nowhere!"

The crowd began to mill as all tried to get back through the barracks door at once. Stefan, imprisoned in the crowd, allowed himself to be carried along. Inside at last, alarm and confusion. Mothers were calling to their children, men were shouting. Stefan somehow made his way to his bunk. And there sat Granny Sophia, her hands serenely folded, her eyes closed. Her lips were moving.

"Granny! What will we do?"

The old woman opened her eyes, shook her head slightly as her lips continued to move, then shut her eyes once more.

"She's praying again," Stefan said aloud. "At a time like this, she's praying!"

In the next moment, however, the old woman at last made the sign of the cross and opened her eyes. "Why, we'll do nothing, child." She cocked her head and listened. "All the same, they've gone," she said.

But that night, in their turn, came the English Lancasters. Their roar, as they passed overhead, catapulted nearly everyone out of bed. Another moment or two, and they were bombarding Weimar and the munitions dump in the forest all over again. Some bold ones dashed out of the barracks and to a nearby hilltop to watch the bombardment of the city. Stefan, however, lay curled in his bunk, tight as a bug, and refused to budge. There was one hit so close that the entire barracks shook and the tiers of bunks swayed. Stefan only burrowed deeper into the blanket.

By next morning, many in the barracks were determined to leave. Of their acquaintances only Mr. Volodko and Dr. Olha declared that they would stay.

"We will go, Stefko," Stefan's father said.

"But where, Dad? There's nowhere to go!"

"Our friend Behun knows of a town not very far away where we can stay in a hotel. It's a small town with no military installations nearby."

The thought of leaving the camp filled Stefan with dismay. They would be going out among strangers again, into that alien world beyond the fence. All over again he would have to accustom himself to new surroundings, new people, except for Martin and his mother. For, without any discussion of the matter they, apparently, were expecting to go with them.

As they packed, Granny Sophia sat unusually quiet after her morning prayer, watching the activity around her. The head kerchief that she wore indoors and out had slipped off her head onto the back of her neck, revealing her thin gray hair done up in a scraggly knot at the back of her head. Suddenly, with a convulsive gesture, she covered her face with her hands.

"Okh, my children," she wailed, rocking back and forth, "how can I bear it! I can't any more."

Startled, everyone turned and stared. Then Mrs. Natalia flew to her. "Granny! What is it? What is it, dear heart?"

"Don't leave me," the old woman whimpered. "Oh, please, not any more. . . ."

Stefan was shocked by the sudden weakness of her voice.

"But Granny . . ." Mrs. Natalia stopped and

75

glanced swiftly toward Stefan's father, her dark eyes asking a large question. Then she knelt beside the old woman. "Why, Granny," she said, her voice thin, "who's leaving you? Impossible! We need you!" She stood and held the old woman's head against her breast, stroking her hair. "We need you," she repeated in a whisper.

Glancing at his father, Stefan saw his eyes kindle, as he stood gazing at the two women. Then his father said, "Don't you stir, Granny! We'll pack your things for you." He laughed and winked. "We're experts! Aren't we, Stefko?"

At last, after good-bys to Dr. Olha, Mr. Volodko, Olexa and his parents, and others, they set forth into the cold for the village, where they would take a train to their destination. As they passed through the gates, Stefan permitted himself a single backward look. Though he had known quite well that they could not stay here forever, during these past weeks—without his willing it—it had become something like home to him. Whenever, after an absence, he had trudged back with Martin and come within sight of this camp, he had hastened his steps like a horse approaching his stable. Within was unquestioned welcome, food, warmth, the company of familiar people—even if not of his own choosing—a bunk to bed down in, a place to keep one's possessions without fear of theft. In a word, home.

And then, there was the house of the accordion. . . .

His father, carrying the valise, turned around. "Come along, Stefko. Don't lag."

Stefan shouldered his pack and fell in beside Granny Sophia. To his relief Martin walked with the other grown-ups, leading the way. Usually so talkative, Granny Sophia only plodded along in silence, keeping her eyes to the road at her feet, never glancing up at the passing scene. Nor did Stefan. He was too numb to care. He was hungry, too, for they had not taken the time for breakfast.

It was not even an hour past sunrise. During the night, a hard frost had settled on the land and now a sharp wind blew. Yet now and again, as Stefan trudged along hunched against it, he thought he detected a vagrant whiff of moist brown earth in the air.

Granny Sophia must have sensed it, too, for suddenly she looked up and said, "The battle between old woman Winter and the maiden that is Spring has already begun, you know. On a day like this one feels it. Back and forth they will do battle, sometimes the old woman winning, sometimes the maiden. Day after day, the battle will rage. But, in the end, Spring will triumph. And she will come bearing gifts for each of us. . . ." She stopped and sighed. "At least, so we old ones say," she added, and fell silent.

Stefan could only shake his head in amusement at the old woman's fancy. What gift would the springtime bring him? What could it bring? The things he wanted most—as soon wish for bird's milk.

Soon enough, they reached the little depot in the village. Across the tracks, Stefan could see the train of boxcars where his father and Mr. Behun had worked. Mr. Behun waved a hand in easy farewell. "Let the Germans finish the job themselves," he said.

A passenger train was standing on the tracks, as if awaiting especially them. Miraculously, after buying their tickets, they all found seats. But it was a long time before the train started, and by the time it did it was packed to the doors, not only with foreign refugees like themselves but Germans as well. Stefan, leaning back in his corner, eyes shut, withdrew from everything. Though he heard voices talking about the air raids of the day before, he scarcely listened.

When, at last, the train began to move, it went at no more than a snail's pace, as if feeling its way blindly along in darkness. After traveling only a short distance, it stopped again. And so through the day: for every few kilometers forward, the train stood on the tracks for hours at a time.

All day long, Stefan alternately dozed and stared out of the window. They were passing hilly, wooded countryside, open fields and extensive orchards spread across broad valleys. In spite of Granny Sophia's prediction of the victory of spring, all was brown and sere.

Several times, Martin, sitting beside him, tried to strike up a conversation with him. But by now Stefan was too disheartened to talk, too confused and too overwhelmed by the sudden turn of events. Once, Martin said in a low voice, "If I've done something, Stefko, I'm sorry."

"It's nothing," Stefan replied, not knowing how else to answer.

78

If they were still back at the barracks—those barracks that had come to mean home—he might, in time, have been able to bring his thoughts together and slowly resume his friendship with Martin. But here they were, he and his father, wandering again. Homeless.

At long last, at a sign from Mr. Behun, they prepared to get off. By now the train was so crowded that they could only inch their way along the corridor to the door. But they all managed to reach it just as the train came to a halt. As soon as the doors opened, they jumped down onto the platform and under a sky gray with snow. The chill wind swept them together like autumn leaves.

Mrs. Natalia laughed. "Spring . . . with a gift of snow!"

"Come!" Mr. Behun commanded them. "It's not far."

As they hurried along, with Mr. Behun in the lead, Stefan could see that he had brought them to a sizeable town. But what with the wind blowing harder and harder, this was no time to linger and look.

"Lord in heaven," Granny Sophia murmured, "where will we lay our heads this night?"

"The proprietress of the hotel I have in mind," Mr. Behun told them, "is a great smoker. For a few cigarettes a day from each of us, she will let us stay as long as our cigarettes last."

The hotel Mr. Behun had in mind was not far from the railroad station. Hurrying against the wind, they reached it in only a few minutes. They crowded through the door and, under cover at last, stood within the doorway for a moment to catch their breath, smooth their hair, and exchange little smiles of triumph among themselves. In the tiny lobby, Stefan saw a woman seated behind a counter. She eyed them for several moments, then came from behind the counter and hurried toward them, a frown on her face.

"No Ostlanders here!" she cried. "No Ostlanders!" Then she pointed up the street. "There's a hotel up there for such as you."

Mr. Behun stepped forward, an ironical smile playing at the corners of his lips. "But madam, we can pay."

The woman only shook her head, stubbornly repeating, "No Ostlanders!"

Mr. Behun, digging into his coat pocket, brought out a packet of cigarettes. They were the Juno brand. "As you see," he murmured.

The woman paused and looked around at them. "But I can only accommodate three," she said.

"Aha! Well, in that case—" Mr. Behun began.

"In that case," Stefan's father put in, "let the women and Martin stay here, while we go up the street to the other hotel. It won't do for them to tramp about in this cold."

And so it was decided. "We'll come back to you in the morning," Stefan's father promised as they parted company.

Half an hour later, in what seemed to be a warehouse district, they found the place the woman had spoken of. It was another small hotel, its windows gray and all but opaque with grime. Chilled to the marrow, they burst inside.

Here a man sat behind the counter. And this time there seemed to be no question about their reception. As Stefan stood waiting for the two men to complete the arrangements, he held each breath for as long as he could to keep from breathing in the stink of stale tobacco smoke and of disinfectant usual in public toilets. From somewhere down the length of a dark corridor leading toward the back of the building came a rumble of male voices. Someone in that direction was plucking at a stringed instrument of some sort, and a wavering female voice was singing.

In a few moments, the three of them made their way down that same corridor. As they passed the open rooms, in nearly every one Stefan caught glimpses of men sitting at cards in a thick haze of smoke, talking and arguing in a tongue he had never heard before. He caught glimpses of women, too.

In a daze he followed his father into a small room lined with triple-decker bunks. One of the tiers was empty. "You'd better take the top bunk, Stefko," his father said.

Without a word, Stefan crawled into the top bunk and, without undressing, lay down. He fell asleep at once.

Soon he was in an enormous cave, the depths of which were alive with a great pack of wolves. "All the wolves of the world have come together," his mother's voice sounded in his ear. All howled their homeless, lonely, heartrending song across an empty world.

A woman appeared and mouthed something. He strained to hear but could not make out the words. All the same, he felt compelled to walk among the wolves, and he realized then that they were all howling at him.

The woman vanished. Was it his mother? He could hear her footsteps crunching on the gravel floor toward the entrance of the cave, but he could no longer see her.

He tried to run after her, calling, "I'm coming! I'm coming!"

But now he discovered that he could not move his feet. Looking down, he saw a thick rope around one ankle. But his other ankle was free. Why couldn't he run? "I'm coming! I'm coming!" he called.

Then a man's voice, from another world, spoke close to his ear. "Come along, then! Hurry!"

He opened his eyes.

"Hurry!" his father repeated, as he picked up his valise.

Swiftly, without question, like an automaton Stefan jumped down from his bunk and followed his father and Mr. Behun out of the room, down the corridor, and out of the building.

eight

OUTDOORS THE SIRENS WERE HOWLING TO THE VERY heavens. The streets lay in darkness, but powerful eyes were sweeping across the skies. A relentless drone, rapidly growing to a roar, made an undersong. Hastily, the three of them fell in with dark, unknown figures silently running down the street.

Some distance to their right a brilliant fountain of light burst into the air with an explosive roar as the first bombs came whistling down to earth. "This way!" someone shouted.

Carrying the valise, Stefan's father struggled to keep up as they ran. "Run on!" he shouted at last.

Mr. Behun hurried on but, as for Stefan, the very thought of being separated from his father only increased his terror. "Dad!" he screamed through the wailing of the sirens. "Leave it! Leave the valise!"

"I can't! Run on!"

In an agony of indecision, Stefan stood for an instant or two, his pounding heart all but bursting through his chest. Then he turned and fled headlong. At last he reached a sizeable building and there, at its door, stood Mr. Behun. Beside him a warden, waving his stick, kept repeating "In here! In here!" garnering all who came fleeing toward him out of the dark.

"He's coming!" Stefan shouted.

But it seemed forever before he saw his father's figure struggling out of the gloom at last. Together they ran down narrow concrete steps and, at the bottom, found themselves in a small room lined with benches on which a few men were seated. Stefan's father, his chest heaving from the effort, asked, "But where are the others? Mrs. Natalia and the others?"

"There must be another shelter, closer to their hotel," Mr. Behun replied as he found them places on one of the benches. "Don't worry, my friend!"

Stefan flung himself down beside his father and sat staring dumbly at the floor. Even within the shelter they could feel the "bukh! bukh!" of the bombs, falling somewhere close by. But if you counted to eight, then you were safe—until the next two clusters of four came dropping down from the skies. For some reason, this bit of handy wisdom, which Stefan had gained from Martin, helped to calm him.

Now and again the shelter itself seemed to shake. His father put an arm around his shoulders. "We'll protect each other," he said, looking down at Stefan with a weary smile.

84

Shutting his eyes, Stefan made no reply, but sat with his body tensed against the thuds of the explosions. He kept his eyes closed the entire time until, at last, after what seemed like hours, but was in fact less than half an hour, the sound of the "all clear" signal reached them. Rousing, mechanically Stefan followed his father and Mr. Behun up the steps and out.

Outdoors, fires flared against the sky in every quarter, rivaling the dawn. The caterwauling of frantic bells and sirens filled the air as fire trucks and ambulances strove to shove their way through the fresh debris of ruined buildings. The whole city seemed wide awake.

"We're in a warehouse district, that's why," his father said, as if in answer to some question in his mind. "The other place, where we left our friends . . ." He broke off and said no more.

Because of the new-laid rubble, they had to move out into the street to make their way, and in some places had to climb over heaps of still smoking ruins. Long tongues of flame, audibly snapping and crackling above the noise, licked at the buildings before devouring them. Sweating and shouting, fire fighters hurried to attach hoses.

Following close on his father's heels past the burning buildings, Stefan remembered how, in Ukrainian towns and villages, he had seen German soldiers look with studied unconcern while women and old men and children fought in vain against flames that were destroying their homes. Now he tried with the same indifference to look upon the men struggling to gain control of the flames.

Miraculously, when they reached their hotel, they found the shabby structure still standing, almost lone among the ruins. But Stefan's father did not go in. He set down his valise, and said, "Take this and wait for me inside, Stefko. Guard it well. I'm going to the other hotel to find our friends."

"I'll go with you," Mr. Behun said.

"Dad, don't go!" Stefan cried. "Don't go!"

But his father only seized him by both shoulders and, giving him a shake, said, "Keep hold of yourself, Stefko. I'll be back, never fear."

And with that, he and Mr. Behun turned and were gone.

In the room, Stefan stowed his father's valise in the lower bunk, flung himself beside it, and fell into an exhausted sleep. He woke to the sound of Mr. Behun's voice. "Come, don't grieve, my friend. We'll find them soon. Just be thankful that they weren't caught under that heap of rubble."

"But where could they have gone?" Stefan's father asked.

"Not far, I assure you. We'll continue our search at once. So take heart, my friend."

Stefan stared at his father, who was sitting on the edge of the opposite bunk, his elbows on his knees, his head in his hands. Frightened by this unusual show of despair, Stefan had only one thought in his head. "But what about me?"

nine

FOR THREE DAYS THEY REMAINED IN THE BOMBED city while Stefan's father, with Mr. Behun's help, searched for the Stefanyks and Granny Sophia. Fortunately, probably because of the worsening winter weather, the Flying Fortresses and the Lancasters did not come again.

Left to himself, Stefan remained in the hotel, guarding his father's valise. He had no desire to risk going outdoors. Day and night, he could still hear the fire alarms resounding through the city, sometimes distant, sometimes close by. But he had seen enough of ruined cities to last him a lifetime. Instead, he spent much of his time dozing in his bunk. Sometimes, he read out-of-date newspapers—laboriously spelling out the German words—that he found in the lobby.

At other times, he even ventured to sit in the lobby

for a while in one of the overstuffed chairs covered with dirty velour that smelled of dust. The air was filled with cheerful waltzes, coming over the radio that the man at the desk kept going nearly all day long. The music was punctuated by occasional war bulletins, but to these Stefan automatically shut his ears.

On the third day of their stay, Stefan's father and Mr. Behun came back earlier than usual. One glance at his father's face told Stefan that his despair had lifted.

"Our friends are alive, Stefko!" his father exclaimed. "At least they're alive!"

Hearing this, Stefan felt a natural relief. But it was a relief mixed with dismay. "But . . . but where are they?" he blurted.

"In a town not very far west of here. They were sent there to an OST camp the morning of the bombing. And we ourselves will follow them, first thing in the morning."

"And none too soon!" Mr. Behun declared. "For the weather will clear and we'll have more bombardments here."

That night, after a supper of bread and cheese in their room, they went to sit in the lobby for a time. A few others were sitting in the plush chairs. The black curtain covering the single large window and the sparse dim lights gave the lobby a murky, cavelike air. But the waltzes were still going full blast.

Suddenly, the music stopped and a German voice came on. "In numerous sectors," the voice announced, "our glorious troops have succeeded in pushing the enemy forces back across the Oder and have taken new positions before Berlin."

Startled as from a deep sleep, every head in the lobby went up. Berlin! But that's not three hundred kilometers away! The bulletin was repeated, and then the music began again in the middle of a phrase. All over the lobby talk suddenly buzzed, like a disturbed hive of bees.

"What does it mean, Dad?" Stefan asked. "I didn't even know they'd crossed the Oder."

"That's just it, Stefko. It's their backhanded way of telling us that the Soviets have crossed and will soon be standing before Berlin. It's catastrophe," he went on. "If the Soviets overrun Germany, we're done for!"

"But will the Americans let them?" Mr. Behun asked. "They can't! We're counting on them!"

Early next morning, the three of them left the hotel and, picking their way through the city, set forth for the town where the Stefanyks and Granny Sophia had gone before them. "We must move westward now, in any case," Stefan's father said, as if making an excuse for following them. "Always westward. Remember that, Stefko."

This time there was no thought of taking a train. Tracks were out all along the line, and, besides, the railroad station was packed with refugees waiting for the next train—any train.

"It's faster walking," Stefan's father said, shifting his valise to his other hand.

"And more pleasant," Mr. Behun added.

Stefan had to admit that this was true, for there was a new hint of spring in the air. Though the acrid smell of charred wet wood hung in the air hovering over the city, now and again Stefan felt fresh, mild puffs of wind against his face as they picked their way among the ruins. He recalled Granny Sophia's description of the coming of spring as a battle between an old woman and a young maiden. By her words, had she invoked that young maiden?

But now another thought came to him. "If the weather is good, they'll come back, won't they?" he asked.

"Who? Oh, you mean the Flying Fortresses," Stefan's father replied. "Who knows? If the weather is good . . ."

"What a pity," Mr. Behun said, "that we must now regret the springtime."

Along with other refugees, they tramped that day over hill, over dale. About mid-afternoon, as they were following a road that led through thick forest, the sky darkened and a wet snow began to fall. When it began to snow harder and harder, they left the road and took to the forest where they would be better protected.

The smell of fungus that pervaded the forest reminded Stefan of his giant mushroom, and that, in turn, of the pictures taken on that occasion. Maybe his father would recall the pictures, especially the one of his mother.

"Dad," Stefan said, "remember that big cauliflower mushroom I found when I was a little kid?"

His father laughed. "Of course, Stefko! And I remember how you bawled when your mother cut it up for drying." He turned to Mr. Behun. "This enormous cauliflower mushroom—sparassis crispa—and he wanted to keep it forever!"

The two men laughed.

Another half hour and they found the OST camp at last. But when Stefan's father inquired at the registry office, he was told that though the Stefanyks and Granny Sophia had indeed registered at the camp, they had already moved on.

"But where?"

"Who knows?"

That day marked the beginning of a long, seemingly endless trek up and down middle Germany from town to town, hostel to hostel and camp to camp. The bombardments had begun again, more relentless than ever. And now and again—from somewhere far off—came a new sound in the land, but one already familiar to Stefan: the song of cannon. As more and more towns came under attack, the roads swarmed alive with refugees, not only foreign ones like themselves, but now Germans also, fleeing Weimar, Dresden, Cologne, Hamburg, even Berlin.

The Germans, of course, were taken in by their own. But nowhere were the foreigners permitted to settle, except in some OST camp or hostel. And these were always dirty, ridden with vermin, and overcrowded. Sometimes they were turned away even from these.

So Stefan and the two men slept in a different place nearly every night, wherever the homeless were permitted to stop and find shelter for a time. But after only a night or two, they were ordered to move on. Now and again, Stefan's father asked him to carry the valise for a short distance. "To give me a breather," he said.

Stefan did so, but he was always glad when he was relieved of that added burden.

Sometimes, for respite, they took a train. Train travel was cheap; for a few marks, they could ride, warm and asleep, clear across Germany. But no matter where they got off, they were met at the station by police who demanded to see their documents. Over and over again, their papers were checked and validated by alert officials in uniform, each wearing an identical mask, forbidding and stern. One night, when they had succeeded in renting a room in a private house, where they thought they could at last stay for a while, the police burst in upon them, demanded their documents, and then warned them to leave by daybreak.

"Having created us," Mr. Behun later remarked drily, "they now fear us."

"All the same, they could still round us up and put us into one of their concentration camps, my friend," Stefan's father pointed out. "So let's be on our guard."

Every place they stopped, Stefan's father asked

about the Stefanyks and Granny Sophia. Always the answer was no . . . no . . . no. Standing by, listening, Stefan sometimes had a secret impulse to repeat his father's words, "Plant a cross upon yesterday."

Of course he did not dare. But he allowed himself a sweet sense of something like revenge. "It's not so easy, is it, old man?" he wanted to say.

But, one day, in a village somewhere in the Thuringian Forest, came news of a sort at last. In a hostel where they were spending the night, they met with some Ukrainians they had known in the camp near Weimar. When Stefan's father asked his perennial question, head shaking was, as usual, the only answer he got.

But overhearing his inquiry, one woman, unknown to them, suddenly spoke up. "Wait! Did that old woman have very blue eyes?"

"Yes!"

"And the young one very dark ones . . . with an almost grown son? But I saw them! I saw them, dear sir!"

"Where? When? Tell me where!"

"It was . . . akh, who knows? Somewhere along the way we saw such a trio . . . about ten days since. Just let me think. . . ."

In the end, however, no matter how she searched and racked her memory, the woman could not recall where she had seen Martin and his mother and Granny Sophia.

All the same, this tenuous news seemed to hearten Stefan's father. "At least they're still alive!" he said.

In the weeks that followed, unable to settle anywhere, they continued to trudge from one town and village to another, one place of refuge to another. Once, in a town somewhere near the Bavarian border, they met with Mr. Volodko. But they spent only the evening together and, in the morning, they parted. Mr. Volodko was on his way to a town somewhere in Bavaria, where a committee was to meet to organize help for the Ukrainian refugees.

More and more often these days, as they skirted the forests of Thuringia, they glimpsed gray figures stealing away through the trees by ones and twos. Only a glimpse, then they vanished from sight.

"Pay them no attention," Stefan's father said. "They're only soldiers taking a short cut home . . . home from the wars." He laughed.

"The German Army—the vaunted Wehrmacht—is rotting from within, it seems," Mr. Behun remarked.

During those days, in Stefan's thoughts the camp near Weimar began to shine as a kind of bright paradise. He forgot all about the bedbugs, the harsh woman in the mess hall, even the sinister forest and all that it might contain. To his chagrin, every time he thought of that camp now, a small painful lump began to form in his throat. Crazy, he told himself angrily, crazy to keep thinking of that miserable camp as home. But he could not help himself.

It was not only the hopeless wandering and the bombing. Hunger stalked the land, too. More and more often, they came upon people—Germans as well as foreigners—rooting in old potato fields after whatever might have been overlooked during the previous harvest.

Food was a constant problem for them, too. Whenever they came to a town or village, they searched out the market square to barter for something to eat.

One day, while the two men were canvassing a village market for bargains in food, Stefan wandered off by himself. He moved from stall to stall, enjoying the stir and the sound of the marketplace, savoring, if only by sight, the foodstuffs laid out. Farmers had come with baskets of wizened winter apples, the bottom of the barrel. There were a few eggs to be had, some cabbages and turnips, and even a little milk.

As at home—perhaps as everywhere in the world—the farm women stood, big dirty aprons across their ample stomachs, well bundled in sweaters underneath. Come winter, come summer, they were always well bundled.

Stefan paused in front of a display of apples, his eyes searching out the biggest one. If he were buying, that would be the one he'd choose. As he stood there, he became aware of the conversation of the stall keeper with her neighbor. "I hear," she was saying, "that the Hauser boy has come home."

"Wounded?"

"No, not wounded. . . ."

"Oh, then . . ."

"Sh! The boy's listening."

"Oh, he's only one of those . . . you know."

"Yes, but watch out for them, in case matters go to the worst."

Stefan wandered on. Apparently, many people had exhausted their cash, or perhaps by now sellers were shunning it as unreliable. Whichever it was, nearly everywhere barter was in full swing. Little groups clustered around the stalls to bargain or listen to others. Stefan found his father and Mr. Behun.

"How much for that sausage?" his father asked the stall keeper.

"What have you got?" the farm woman asked, suspicion in her eyes.

"Cigarettes." His father held up a pack of Juno's. "Ten of those."

"For one kilo? That's dear!"

But for some brands, like the cheap "Sport" variety, he would have had to give a whole pack. And there were still some who refused to accept that brand at all.

Bars of precious soap—most of it American Army soap, wherever that had come from!—were traded for a fowl or a piece of salt pork or some smoked fish. What would they give for the bar of fine English toilet soap that Stefan carried in his pack? He grinned. The entire stall, no doubt! And suddenly he felt rich, far above all this mean and grudging bargaining.

ten

AT LAST, ONE DAY, NOT KNOWING ANY LONGER WHERE
to go, Stefan and the two men took a train that happened to be standing in the station of the nameless
town where they had spent the night and rode to some
equally nameless destination. When, toward the end
of the day, they got off the train, they learned that
for a few marks they had traveled southward clear
athwart Germany and, at this moment, were within
hail of the Swiss frontier.

As they stood for a moment gazing hungrily toward
that frontier, Stefan could see the border guards moving about. *"Ave atque vale. . . ."* Mr. Behun murmured.

Hail and farewell! And so they turned their backs
on the unattainable and set forth through the town
in search of lodging. It was already turning dusk and

they had not gone far when, to their amazement, the street lights went on.

Turn them off! Turn them off, you fools! Stefan wanted to shout the alarm.

But the lights burned brightly on, as if the townspeople were oblivious of the Europe that lay in darkness all around them. Fearfully, as if some catastrophe was about to strike as a result, Stefan walked along almost tiptoeing at his father's heels. The town itself stood quite untouched by war, as untouched as seemingly its people were.

"Here we'll stay, my friends!" Mr. Behun cried, speaking for all three.

It must have been the supper hour, for the little streets were deserted. They walked a considerable distance toward the center of town before they saw anyone. It was a policeman. Approaching them, he stopped and blocked their way. "Documents, please."

Stefan breathed a sigh of relief. This, at least, was familiar.

"By tomorrow morning," the policeman was saying as he handed back their papers, "you will take your leave. Your papers do not permit you to stay more than one night."

"Understood," Mr. Behun said in that affable tone of his, "but can we not get fresh permits to stay on?"

"Under no circumstances. Foreigners are permitted to stay here only overnight."

"But where will we go?" Stefan blurted in German.

"Where did you come from? Weimar? Go there!"

And with that the policeman pointed his stick in the direction of the railroad station they had left only a little while before. He stood waiting as they shouldered their packs and turned about to retrace their steps.

As they walked silently along, each no doubt thinking the same wounded thoughts, Stefan stole a glance at his father. The lines of bitterness about his mouth seemed to have deepened. He wondered whether he looked like that, too. It was a long time since he had seen himself in a mirror.

As if to compound their misery, they had not gone far before a cold rain began to fall. Stefan, hurrying to keep up, had only one thought in his head: shelter. Shelter from this miserable rain, shelter from the wretched world. He wanted to crawl into a hole somewhere and hide from everyone and everything. But where? He stared somberly down the wet, empty street lined with its tidy little houses. Even the fox in the woods has his lair. . . .

His steps began to lag. He stared at his father's back, but he was too despondent for anger.

And precisely here is where the miracle came to pass. They were trudging along the narrow street that they had traversed only a little while before when, suddenly, the door of a house they were passing opened. A woman appeared in the doorway and, as Stefan glanced in her direction, she beckoned to him.

Seeing this, his father gave him a little push. "Go.

See what she wants. I'll take your pack. We'll walk slowly on and you can catch up."

Obediently Stefan gave up his pack and ran over to the woman. Taking him by the arm, she drew him inside. *"Bitte,"* she said.

Within, Stefan found himself in a rather small, low-ceilinged room, filled with so many things that he hardly knew where to look first. There were rich carpets on the floor, a sofa with a faded cloth that looked like tapestry thrown over it, a table with a lighted lamp on it. There were some books, oil paintings on the walls, and in a corner a large tile stove, glowing with heat. So this is how they lived, the capitalists of the western world. Stefan had never seen such luxury.

He had not been inside a real home since . . . since Poltava. A long forgotten feeling came stealing over him that he could not name—of comfort, of security, of warmth. Yes, surely warmth. . . .

But he had no more time to gaze about, for the woman, pointing to a coat that was draped over a chair in front of the table, was making gestures for him to put it on. When Stefan hesitated, not sure what her purpose was, she picked up the coat and held it up, inviting him to slip his arms into the sleeves.

He did so. It fit. And it was warm. True, the edges of the sleeves were well worn. But the coat was warm.

Then, shaking his head resolutely, he began to take it off. No, no way could they afford such a luxury.

"Nein! Nein!" the woman exclaimed, pulling the coat back onto him.

100

He tried to explain, but apparently his German was not adequate. At last he thought to reach into one of his jacket pockets and turn it inside out to show that he had no money. As if to emphasize the gesture, the pocket even had a hole in it. He looked up at her and grinned.

Talking volubly, she took him by the shoulders, turned him about, and steered him, coat and all, toward the door. Only then did the truth come upon him.

She was giving him the coat. A perfectly good, warm winter coat! Now she was thrusting him out through the door, nodding and smiling and making reassuring sounds. "But tell no one," she whispered.

That much he understood. "Tell no one."

In his astonishment, all the German that he had so far learned completely deserted him. *"Danke!"* was all that came to his lips. *"Danke!"*

"Remember, no one!" the woman repeated, her finger to her lips.

Instinctively Stefan understood. He was not to tell any townspeople of her generous gift, else they might make trouble for her.

"Danke!" he cried again. Then he turned and raced after his father and Mr. Behun.

The two men were as astounded by the gift as he, but each found a different meaning in it. "Her conscience hurt her," Mr. Behun remarked.

"Well, then we can credit her with that much," Stefan's father countered drily. "Maybe it belonged to her son when a boy," he went on. "Probably killed

101

on the eastern front by now. Or, what's worse, taken prisoner by the Reds, poor devil." He paused for a moment, then added, "Or maybe she's trying to buy her way out of the retribution every one of them has earned."

"On the other hand, my friend," Mr. Behun put in, "let's not be so suspicious as all that. We're not back among the Soviets, you know. Maybe it was just a simple gift, given out of the goodness of the human heart." He paused, then added, "Sometime, before doomsday catches up with us, we'll all have to forgive each other, however grudgingly."

Stefan glanced up at him.

"What, Stefko, you don't believe me?" Mr. Behun asked in a bantering tone.

Stefan only smiled from the depths of his warm coat. It seemed an odd remark. Perhaps that is why he remembered it.

"The goodness of the human heart," his father murmured. "Yes, there's that. There is that. . . ."

They spent that night on a train going back north into Thuringia. Sitting snug and warm under cover of the coat, Stefan sleepily pondered the gift. All right, so once in a blue moon you came upon someone who showed kindness for secret reasons of his own. The kindness wasn't supposed to be, just as water is never supposed to flow upward. But people are flesh, not water, and they simply do not always act in accord with the rules. And that is that.

There was the German tankman who had given them a lift in his tank, somewhere on the road out

102

of Lwiw, under fire and at the risk of severe reprimand, perhaps even worse, from his superior officers. That certainly was at odds. And there was that Czech who had shared his sausage with them on the train from Prague to Dresden, less than two months ago. Before that there was even the Russian soldier with whom they had suddenly come face to face in some woods near Rohatyn in western Ukraine. That one had deliberately looked the other way as they fled through the trees. For that was what a friend often was, not someone who did one a kindness, but someone who did one the least possible harm.

And now this German woman. . . .

Why were people so unpredictable? It was downright disorderly—impossible to sort matters. No doubt, when this war showed up in the history books, future generations of kids would have to learn about it. In Poltava, they'd have to stand beside their desks at stiff attention and recite, "In the year 1941 the Hitlerian Fascists treacherously invaded our glorious Soviet Fatherland. But with the help of our citizenry, who to a man loyally and heroically fought the barbarous invader, in the year . . ."

When? When would it all end?

It would appear ever so neat and orderly—for only orderly wars are fought in history books—with dates fore and aft to box them nicely in. But everyone who had been there would know it all for a lie. Because the truth was anarchy and chaos, friends where enemies should be and enemies among one's own. . . .

eleven

Yet, if it had not been for his perennial hunger and for having to tramp about burdened with luggage, particularly that valise of his father's sometimes, by now Stefan might have found travel along the Thuringian countryside even pleasant. For the sweet month of April was on its way. Thaw had set in and the earth was sending forth the warm green exhilarating smell of life renewing itself. Everywhere people were out, working in the fields and orchards.

At home by now, after the long winter would come days when they could leave off their caps and snow boots, and go about with their jackets thrown open to the spring sun. Pavlo would be getting out his soccer ball—not to play, for the lot where they usually played would still be under at least a foot of hard-packed snow. But just to bounce it around a bit in the apartment.

On second thought . . . on second thought, erase that picture. For who knew whether the apartment house was still standing? Who knew whether Pavlo was even alive? For in their headlong retreat out of Ukraine, the Nazis, just as the Soviets had done, had in their turn left ruin and fresh corpses behind them —in Poltava as well, probably.

Here, in Germany, too, in spite of the spring, they had to force their thoughts back to the world at war. The two men, especially, were shaken by the fear that the Soviet Army, now that it was invading Germany, might indeed overrun the region of their refuge. Daily they sought out the latest news.

More than once, they stopped to talk to OST field hands. Always they inquired about two women, one young, the other old, traveling with a nearly grown boy. Always the answer was no, such a trio had not been seen. Usually, too, they asked whether their masters might be in need of extra hands.

"In return for our keep," Stefan's father said, "we'll gladly turn our hands to any kind of work—any work at all."

To this, too, the answers were always no. Their masters already had more help than they knew what to do with.

But one day, after the three of them had slept the previous five nights in five different places, their luck took another turn. It happened near a town on the western edge of Thuringia. Walking along the well-paved road, they were approaching a big farmhouse built of stone, surrounded with numerous barns and sheds, and standing some distance off the road. Coming abreast of the place, at the roadside they saw a pretentiously tall wrought-iron gate in front of it. But though the gate was closed, it stood alone, without a sign of fence.

They stood eyeing the house. "Look," Stefan said, "a stork's nest on the chimney top."

"That's a good sign," Mr. Behun said. "Let's try in here."

So they walked around the gate and up the narrow road toward the house. As they approached, a girl came out of one of the barns carrying a pail in either hand. She was wearing an OST armband. Seeing them, she stopped and gazed at them curiously.

Stefan's father approached her. "Good day, miss," he said in German. "May we speak to your master?"

"What about?"

But her accented German evidently gave his father a clue, for now he answered the girl in Ukrainian.

"Okh!" she cried, sudden gladness in her eyes. "Where are you from . . . where from?" She set down her pails.

Mr. Behun spoke up. "I'm from Drohobych and my friends . . ."

"But that's not far from my home!" she cried. "What news of home? Oh, what news?"

"Ah, dear child, who knows? We left home months ago . . . and a lot has happened since then . . ."

Yes. A lot.

Her name was Olenka, she told them, and her

106

master had also a Pole as well as two Lithuanians working for him.

Then Stefan's father asked his usual question: two women and a boy?

No, Olenka shook her blonde head. No. She picked up the pails again. "But if you're looking for a place for the night, or for something to eat, it'll do you no good to ask my master. That one's the devil's own sire and his wife the devil's own dam! As it is, they're being plagued to death by all the people on the road now . . . and lately they have been turning away even their own."

As they stood talking, the door of the house opened and a large woman stood in the doorway. For a moment she stared hostilely at them, then started toward them with rapid strides.

"See?" the girl murmured. "She's coming to drive you off. But you go hide in the bushes down the road a way. When dusk falls, come back to this same spot and I'll bring you something to eat. Don't be afraid. Their dogs have gone to war."

By this time, the woman was almost upon them. "*Raus! Raus!*" she began to shout, flinging her arms wildly about. "*Raus!*"

The girl scurried away as fast as she could, the empty pails swinging from her hands. Stefan stood plucking at his father's sleeve. "Come on, Dad. It's no use."

Undaunted, his father stepped forward. He bowed. "Madam," he began, "we . . ."

107

But the woman kept shouting, *"Raus! Raus!"*

"Madam," his father began again, "we have only stopped by to ask for work."

The woman paused and looked from one of them to the other. Then she said, "Why don't you people stay where you belong, instead of wandering in others' lands?"

Before this monstrous question, for a moment not even Mr. Behun found words. But then, recovering himself, he said, "Now there's a coincidence, madam! That's the very same question we have been asking . . . only not about ourselves!" He smiled.

"How? What?" she spluttered.

Now it was Stefan's father who plucked at Mr. Behun's sleeve. "Come along, friend. It's useless. Can't you see that the thought has never occurred to her?"

They picked up their luggage and started back for the road. But they had not quite reached it when, from behind them, a man's voice shouted, "Wait!"

They turned. The man stood beckoning to them. As they drew near, he asked, "Do you know forestry work?"

Mr. Behun stepped forward, a wide smile on his face. "Sir, we are born foresters!"

The man eyed him, uncertain. "I need someone to clear brush out of my woodland."

"What a coincidence!" Mr. Behun cried. "That's precisely our specialty! Just show us the woodland and we'll clear it neat as you please!"

Again the man eyed them suspiciously. "There's no cash pay. You can sleep in the cow barn and get two meals a day." He peered at them for their reaction.

"Sybaritic!" exclaimed Mr. Behun.

"But only for as long as the work lasts," the man added. "And the boy must help."

Abruptly the man turned and led the way back toward the farmyard. Picking up their burdens, they hastened after him. When they reached the farmyard again, the man waved an arm toward one of the barns and said, "In there." Then he disappeared into the house.

Stefan followed his father and Mr. Behun into the barn. As he stepped inside, he smelled the warm smell of sweet hay and animals. Each stall was occupied by a cow, except one in which a motorcycle, covered with a piece of tarpaulin, was parked.

"Here's one that's empty," Mr. Behun said. "I suppose he means for us to bed down in there."

The stall was clean and fresh straw was heaped in a corner of it. They set down their luggage and while the two men began to spread the straw for a bed for the three of them, Stefan stepped to the doorway again and looked out. At last he turned and called, "Dad, I'm going out!"

Without waiting for an answer, he bolted through the door and escaped into springtime. For once free of luggage, he galloped twice around the big courtyard, feeling deliciously giddy. Then he ran past the big house toward the outbuildings on the other side. But before he could reach them, he came to an ell in the house—and there stood the master.

Startled, Stefan stopped in his tracks. The man was digging a hole with a spade. Beside him on the ground lay a long thin object and a number of small ones, each wrapped in cloth. Out of one end of the long object, where the cloth did not quite reach, jutted a gun stock.

The man straightened and, seeing Stefan, gave a shout, flourishing the spade like a weapon. Stefan turned on his heel and raced back into the barn. Behind him, the man ran into the courtyard, halted, and once more shouted something. Then he turned and disappeared behind the house again.

"The master here is burying some weapons," Stefan reported.

"Aha," his father remarked, "so they've already smelled their final defeat."

"With their weapons buried," Mr. Behun added, "they'll play as innocent as babes when the Americans come. 'Who, me?' they'll say."

Stefan had to laugh at the mock round-eyed innocence on Mr. Behun's face.

Late that afternoon Olenka came with her pails and began to milk the cows. Afterward, the three of them helped her to bed down the animals for the night. As they worked, they talked.

Her home, she told them, was a small town on the Dnistr River in western Ukraine, and it was now four years since she had been seized and transported to Germany. Her masters were harsh and several of the OST people who had worked for them had run away. At the moment they had only four workers left. But she was the only Ukrainian among them. They all stayed in an outbuilding on the other side of the farmyard.

Suddenly, as she spoke, she paused and looked up. Tears came welling into her eyes and quietly she began to cry. "This is the first time I've spoken in my own tongue for nearly a year," she moaned softly.

They looked at her for a moment, not knowing what to do. Then Stefan's father, standing beside her, drew her to him, stroked her head, and murmured, "Weep all you wish, dear child. You're among your own now. Soon it will be over and you will go home at last."

Later that evening the girl came back with their supper, some bread and yellow cheese that had grown so stale and hard that it was almost impossible to bite into it. "The mistress says since you have not yet done any work for them, this is all she can spare. But I brought you this."

And, with a secret smile, she delved into her apron pocket and brought out a piece of sausage. "The mistress miscounted them the other day . . . and this was left over. It's cooked, so eat!"

As they ate, she talked. "My master's son," she said, "is home from the wars. But I think he's deserted, for he stays in the attic and never ventures out. I have not seen him, but several times a day the mistress goes up to the attic, where she never went before." She laughed. "They speak a bit more civilly to us now.

111

And one day the mistress even gave me this old skirt of hers, with the words, 'No need to speak of our guest, my dear.'"

"I caught your master burying some guns," Stefan said.

"Aha!" Olenka exclaimed. "So that's what they were whispering about this morning."

At last, from the direction of the house, came a sudden shout. Hastily, the girl got to her feet. "I must go quickly, else she'll come after me. She's worried I'll tell what I know. You are to be ready for work by daylight, the master said."

She turned and hurried out of the barn. In the next moment came an angry torrent of words, the sound of a door slammed . . . and silence.

Stefan, his stomach pleasantly full for once, lay back on the straw and, using his coat for a blanket, he closed his eyes. Taking deep breaths of the sweet smell of hay, he listened to the cozy sound of the cows as they chewed their cud and he felt a magical comfort.

As he drowsed off to sleep, he thought briefly of the harsh masters of this place. At least they behaved in the manner appropriate to them—one had to give them that. Turning over on his side, sleepily he smacked his lips. Yes, in a twisted sort of way, all was right with his nightmare world.

twelve

AFTERWARD, EACH SMALLEST EVENT OF THAT MORN-
ing was indelibly imprinted upon Stefan's memory.
Olenka came before dawn to awaken them and bring
them breakfast. Stefan's father asked her where he
might keep his valise safe during their absence at
work.

"Why, right here in the stall, sir," she replied.
"I'm almost the only one who comes into this barn.
Set it in the corner there and heap some straw over
it. It will be safe enough."

But his father was not assured by this casual sug-
gestion. After the girl left, he climbed up into the
loft with the heavy valise and there, among the rafters,
he found a good hiding place for it.

A little later, one of the OST farmhands came into
the barn. "We're to bring out the brushwood," he
said. "Just the four of us."

Then, leading an ox out into the yard, he harnessed it to a wagon. In a little while, they were plodding along the road that would take them to the master's woodland. While the farmhand drove, the three of them sat behind him in the wagon, silent, enjoying the fresh spring morning and the countryside festive with blossoms. It was going to be a fair day, sunny and warm. With the rise of the sun the clouds had dispersed, one by one, leaving a clear deep blue sky overhead. High up there a bird of prey soared on the thermal waves arising from the warming earth. Stefan sat watching it.

On the road up ahead, a wagon train drawn by horses was approaching them. As it neared, moving briskly toward them, they saw that it was a military transport train, so long that they could not see the end of it. It was because of the jingle of gear and the clop-clop of the horses' hoofs on the asphalt that, at first, none of them heard the droning sound in the sky.

Stefan was the first to hear. But, by then, the planes were nearly overhead. In the next instant, they were swooping down, one after another, to the rattle of machine guns.

My God! They're attacking the train! Oh, my God!

Leaping out, they flung themselves under the wagon. Horses screamed as the planes came roaring down upon the wagons, spitting fire. Stefan lay clutching the earth, aware that he was howling into the dirt at the top of his lungs. Somewhere, in the lost mist of the past, was this same moment when he had lain in a ditch beside his father, helpless under the strafing of the metal monsters in the sky.

Then came deathly stillness . . . only for an instant. Somebody moaned. Stefan lifted his head. Beside him, face down, lay his father. "Dad? Dad!"

Blood was rapidly staining his father's jacket. He raised his head, found Stefan, and murmured, "We must begin again." Then he let his head drop back and closed his eyes.

thirteen

AFTER CONSIDERABLE DELAY, THEY TOOK STEFAN'S
father and Mr. Behun, along with the wounded German soldiers, to the hospital in the nearby town.
Gathering up his pack in the cowbarn at the farmhouse, Stefan followed on foot. At the hospital he
waited all that morning long before he received the
word: "Your father has been shot in the lung. Expect
the worst."

Stefan was allowed a brief visit at the bedside, but
his father lay unconscious. The nurse soon told Stefan
to leave.

As for Mr. Behun, his was a leg wound and, though
he had lost much blood, the wound would soon heal.
Stefan waited all day at the hospital for further word
and, when none came, at dusk he shouldered his
pack and left the building.

But he did not go far. For a long time, he stood

in front of the hospital, his pack at his feet, not knowing what to do with himself or which way to go. Back to the farmhouse? Of course not. They had already washed their hands of him, his father, and Mr. Behun.

Then it occurred to him that his father's valise had been left behind in the cowbarn. Here his thoughts came to a long pause.

No, he couldn't face the masters of that farm . . . not today. They were indeed formidable, as Olenka had said. Dragons. And he was no dragon-slayer. He could wait until his father had recovered. Then they would go together, and he would gladly carry the valise for his father. Yes, that made sense. As soon as his father had recovered . . .

How long he stood in front of the hospital he could not have said. For the first time in his life, he was completely on his own . . . and he did not know what to do. More than that, there was a stone in the very pit of his stomach that would not go away.

At last a policeman approached him. Instead of his usual momentary panic, Stefan felt relief. For the hundredth time, "Show me your papers."

"Yes, here they are, sir."

Then, "what are you doing here?"

"My father's in this hospital . . . and I have no-where else to go."

"Come along, then."

That night Stefan found himself in a small school-house near the edge of town that had been turned into a hostel for wanderers like himself. There was the usual noise and continuous stir of people—the usual cacophony of half the tongues of Europe.

Stefan readily found the room and the straw mattress on the floor that had been assigned to him. By now he was adept at such handy little skills. On the adjoining mattress an old man with a rugged, misshapen face sat crosslegged, muttering something to himself over a piece of cloth in his hand. He was plying a needle and when Stefan looked, he saw that the man was embroidering.

As Stefan dropped his pack onto the mattress, the man looked up. Pausing, with needle in midair, he asked, "So you're our new neighbor? But where are your folks?"

"I'm alone."

"Ah, well, so am I. So are we all in this little corner. It's bad." He held up the cloth. "When I yearn for my kinfolk and my village, I embroider. It helps to ease my burden. I embroider and recite Shevchenko's poetry to myself from memory. Where are you from?"

"Poltava, Grandad. And you?"

"From the left bank . . . a little village named Bolotakh. And in truth, in spring especially, it's a regular mudhole!" He smiled, merriment dancing in his eyes. "But as they say, even the mother owl loves her little chicks, ugly though they are. And so it is with my village. But how is it, my son, that a lad like you is wandering the wide world alone?"

Stefan told him.

118

The man shook his head ruefully. "A rum business. So what now?"

Stefan only shrugged his shoulders. He did not want to continue the conversation. His father, if he had been there, would have sat down with the old man and soon made his acquaintance. But not he . . . not any more. He no longer had any appetite —if he ever had—for new faces or new places. He was sick unto death of the life of a nomad.

He lay down and in a few moments fell into a deep, haunted sleep.

By next morning, when he went back to the hospital, his father was gone. He had died just before dawn.

"We would have summoned you, but we did not know where to find you," they told him. "We did warn you, remember!"

"I should have gone after the valise." For some obscure reason, the words "I should have gone . . . should have gone" echoed through Stefan's thoughts.

The unreasonable idea would not leave him that, if only he had gone after the valise and kept it with him, his father would not have died. His father himself must have felt this, known this, for look how he had clung to that valise. For dear life. Without it, he had died . . . and now it was too late.

Afterward, Stefan found it difficult to remember the funeral. Others made the arrangements, and besides himself only strangers attended it. They were people from the schoolhouse who came out of a feeling of loyalty to a compatriot in exile. Mr. Behun was not able to come.

As if to mark that day, though it was April, snow fell and buried the greening earth. Stefan remembered this snow. During the night, frost had blighted the orchards that they passed on the way to the burial ground. Only the day before, the countryside had been fragrant with blossoms; now they had turned brown and were falling from the trees, as if in silent reproach. The fragile young spring that Granny Sophia had evoked had been put to rout.

In the days that followed, Stefan lived in a nightmare from which he was unable to awaken. He heard human voices and understood them, but somehow they failed to penetrate his inner ear. A wall had mysteriously grown up around him, isolating him from everyone and everything. He felt that he was not of the world but in some private limbo not of his own creation.

At home, incredible as it now seemed to him, he used to become annoyed whenever one or the other of his parents had asked him where he was off to. Now no one did. He could come and go as he pleased and no one asked him where he was going, not even old Mr. Kostur, the embroiderer. In the face of this utter freedom, Stefan could only feel a growing terror. He even began to envy some of the young children in the schoolhouse whenever their parents scolded them. As for himself, there was no one to show him, tell him, order him.

Strangers offered him food, consolation, sympathy,

advice. None of it helped. The long empty, aimless days continued to stretch before him like a desert that he must stumble across before night came, when he could at last fall into oblivion again. Among these strangers he could not weep, so the oblivion of sleep was his only relief.

That and old man Kostur. If it were not for him, what would he do? The old man offered him what he had. He even offered to teach him to embroider. "I'll teach you Shevchenko's verses, too," he said. "You have no idea how such things help."

When Stefan only shook his head, the old man said mildly, "Ah, well, each finds his own way," and continued with his work and his whispered recitations.

Stefan, lying on his mattress, did not trouble to unravel the sense of the words that the old man, in a voice now rising, now falling, murmured so persistently. But their rhythm was a lullaby, an incantation that brought him a measure of solace.

It so happened that there was no one Stefan's age in the schoolhouse. But one day, urged by some of the women, Stefan went out among the young children playing in the yard and supervised their games. Their shrill welcome gave him release, but it was only temporary. He was glad enough to return to his mattress, where he lay outstretched as before, his coat for cover, staring wide-eyed at the dirty gray ceiling and marveling at the laughter he heard now and again.

At last one day, old man Kostur began asking him

questions, casually, but genuinely wanting to know about his life in Poltava. Haltingly Stefan began to talk. He even told about the accordion he had left behind. That helped. It helped, too, that the old man, seeming to know just when to take over, in his turn began rambling on about himself. This gave Stefan time to regain control of his voice and then, out of politeness, he even asked a question or two of his own.

After that it was easier. Gradually, Stefan found himself able to think of his father and even to speak of him to old man Kostur without that lump in his throat forming instantly.

There came the day when he began to hear the talk around him. The talk at last had turned to the war. Always the war.

"The Germans have lost," someone said. "The Americans, thank God, will take over. They'll hang Hitler and his gang . . ."

"But what about the Russians?" That came from the youngish man in the corner, the one with the straw-colored hair and the crooked nose whose name was Koval.

"The Russians? How do you mean, the Russians?"

"I mean you think they won't want their share?"

"Of Germany? But that means . . . then what will become of us?"

"Now that's the question!" Koval burst out. "That, brother, is the very kernel of the matter!"

What would his father have said to such an ironical turn of fate, Stefan wondered as he listened, that after all the miles and misery of flight, the very terror they had fled should at last be on the point of catching up with them?

As the days went by, in the schoolhouse curiosity—mixed with not a little fear over the approach of the Americans—grew more intense. A certain curiosity at last began to infect Stefan, too.

He could not decide what to think. Surely of all capitalists in the world, the American was the arch capitalist. And capitalists were cold-blooded, hard-hearted, money grabbing, . . . and too rich. So he had learned at school in Poltava.

But what would the Americans be like in the flesh? He wondered. Would they come like those Red Army units who had marched in to occupy Halych province of western Ukraine, sinister and merciless, as Mr. Behun had once described to them? A raggle-taggle in goose step?

No, more likely they would come roaring in on huge monsters with caterpillar treads and on motorcycles, kicking up great clouds of dust, and swiftly fill the streets with naked force, like the Germans he had watched entering Poltava, nearly four years before.

But days passed and no Americans appeared. Though the skies were alive with their planes, flying singly or in squadrons, they completely bypassed the town.

In the town, people said, the pictures of Hitler

and the swastika insignia that had been everywhere had quietly disappeared from public places. The forests roundabout, they said, were now alive with deserters from the Wehrmacht who were making their way home by the back roads, but scarcely bothering to hide any longer.

And still no Americans.

fourteen

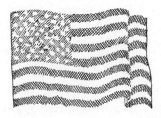

THE SNOW HAD LONG AGO MELTED AND SPRING RE-
turned, boldly this time, prepared to stay. And on a
day late in April, Mr. Behun, his wound healed, was
at last released from the hospital. Though he would
have to walk with a cane for a while, he had recovered
much of his usual good cheer. He took refuge in the
schoolhouse and was assigned a place in what old man
Kostur called "our little corner." And now, at last,
for Stefan there was one "old friend" among the
strangers.

But to his mortification, almost at once Mr. Behun asked about his father's valise. For a startled
moment, Stefan did not know how to answer. He felt
himself growing hot under the collar, as if he had
been caught red-handed in some wrongdoing. He had
completely forgotten the valise. But he could not say
so, nor could he say, "I abandoned it."

"I couldn't carry it and my pack both," he blurted out at last.

"But where is it?" Mr. Behun persisted. "Still at that farmhouse? Aha! You will have to go back for it, my boy. Your father . . ." He broke off and only shook his head.

Stefan avoided Mr. Behun for the rest of that day.

The next morning, without warning, life took yet another sharp turn, erasing the matter of the valise from Stefan's thoughts. Early that morning, some of the children came dashing into the schoolhouse. "They're here!" they shouted, then dashed right out again. Everybody dropped what they were doing and followed them.

"Come, Stefko," Mr. Behun said. "They're here!"

But Stefan was already at the door. Leaving Mr. Behun behind, he ran with the crowd out of the yard and down the street toward the highway.

And there at the end of the little street, blocking the way, stood a vehicle. Not until later did Stefan learn that it was called a "jeep." Lounging in the front seat, his knee cocked against the steering wheel, sat an American soldier. He wore no helmet. Beside him, of equally unmilitary bearing, sat another. Both were slowly chewing something and this gave them an air of colossal self-assurance, as if to say, "Why sweat?" Casually, as if they were watching a show, they gazed toward the highway, along which Stefan now saw tanks and open trucks, filled with soldiers, rumbling swiftly past.

Together, as if seeking safety in numbers, the

crowd from the schoolhouse approached the highway. One of the soldiers in the jeep turned his head and, seeing them, grinned. Stefan for one did not return the smile. No, my fine friend, we'll see what you are first. . . .

When Stefan reached the road, he saw that it was thinly lined with some of the townspeople, watching in glum silence. American flags were fluttering from more than one window along the road. Where on earth had they come from?

But what astonished Stefan was this first sight of the American Army. The soldiers, short rifles in hand, were leaning over the sides of the trucks, casually viewing the passing scene as if they were on a weekend excursion. Some had cigarettes dangling from their lips. Many were chewing something, and this was the final touch that gave such a cool air to this whole invasion.

Stefan could not take his eyes off the soldiers' uniforms, obviously made of the finest wool. And the gear, the tanks, and the trucks—all finished with the high polish of a fine watch. Turning, he stared for a moment at the boots of the two in the jeep. Never in his life had he seen such fine ones. Made of the finest leather, probably, with good thick soles.

Beside him, he now saw, stood Mr. Behun leaning on his cane. He, too, seemed impressed. "An army of aristocrats," he remarked. "Eh, Stefko?"

Stefan gazed at the soldiers' faces, so open, so calm and unconcerned. "I wonder what they're really like?" he said.

"That's to be seen, my boy." Mr. Behun echoed Stefan's own thought.

Stefan had looked into the faces of conquering armies before. But these faces were not those of ordinary conquerors. "I wonder," he asked, "if they've been all through the war—or if they're maybe fresh troops?" Had they ever known anguish, these lithe young men with the open faces?

But Mr. Behun seemed so absorbed in the spectacle before them that he did not answer.

Stefan did not know what to think. He felt a poignant need to talk with somebody—his father—to hear what he would have to say about this momentous occasion and these strange people from another world.

The passing through of the American columns lasted nearly all of that day. And afterward, it was hard to believe that with this single, seemingly casual "parade" of theirs, the Americans had "conquered" the town. It was almost laughable, for they did it without puffing out their chests or strutting about like so many cocks.

"Our true liberators, it seems, have come at last," Mr. Behun remarked.

Stefan spent nearly the whole of that day out on the streets, footloose among the milling crowds. Buoyed by a heady feeling of safety at last, of freedom from fear after years of living in daily and imminent peril, he felt as though his feet were scarcely touching the ground. Judging from the faces and the easy laughter, others apparently shared this feeling of intoxication.

OST laborers, dressed in their best, flaunting their OST armbands upon their chests like so many war decorations, strolled about as if it were some great holiday. Many, the Ukrainians among them, wore embroidered holiday shirts that they had brought to Germany with them as mementoes of home. Some Ukrainians wore bits of blue-and-gold ribbon—their national colors, long forbidden by the Soviets.

Now and again, Stefan came upon mere shadows of men and women who had clearly just been liberated from some nearby concentration camp. They tottered along among the crowds with a certain arrogance that struck Stefan as grotesque. Many of them displayed large red ribbons on their chests.

Stefan came upon a group that surrounded one of these people. They were arguing about something. Seeing Mr. Kostur in the group, he stopped beside him.

In the center of the group, a concentration camp survivor had confronted Koval, their mate from the schoolhouse, who was wearing a bit of blue-and-gold ribbon. "But man, have you gone daft?" Koval was saying. "The Soviets have concentration camps, too. You know that as well as I do! They invented them! So how do you figure that the Soviets are better than . . ."

The concentration camp survivor, fists clenched, shouted in Russian, "Just you wait till they come! I'll turn you all in to the Soviets! Count on it! Traitors!" And he spat.

For a moment, the deadly threat stunned the crowd.

Then, muttering, the group swiftly dissolved. The concentration camp survivor sauntered on, weaving like a reed in the wind.

"Eh, what a rum business," old man Kostur murmured, as they stood watching him disappear into the crowds. "He's gone dotty, poor wretch. All the same," he added, giving Stefan a keen look, "he'd do it . . . turn us all in without a second thought!"

Now a row of girls, arm in arm and laughing, came by, Olenka among them. Catching sight of Stefan, she called as they approached, "Stefan, we're going home!"

"You are?" Stefan could not keep the awe out of his voice.

"Yes . . . as soon as possible! My parents are there, my brother, my sisters. . . ."

"But how do you know?" Stefan asked. "Maybe they're all . . ."

"Hush, don't say it," Mr. Kostur interrupted. "Don't upset the girl."

"Here, by myself," Olenka continued, "I'm an orphan."

"It'll be different at home now," one of the other girls said. "Better! The Americans won't let the Soviets . . ."

This time Mr. Kostur dissented. "No, my dear child, don't dream," he said. "Things will be the same as before. And until they change . . ."

Stefan's heart was pounding wildly. What would it be like to see Pavlo again . . . and the others? What would it be like to walk his own streets again and play soccer in the lot around the corner? For the first time in many a day, the old yearning returned —the unbearable yearning to see Pavlo again, to tell him all he had seen and everything he had lived through. Otherwise, who was there to listen?

He ought to write Pavlo a letter, at once. But, no, he could tell him nothing, even if he wrote. As a matter of fact, he could not write to him at all for he'd only get them all into trouble with the authorities.

That afternoon, every house in town was visited by a squad of American soldiers. One came to the schoolhouse as well, and Stefan crowded in with the others for this first close contact with an American.

Speaking a German no better than theirs, the officer in charge begged everyone's pardon and announced that they would search the premises for weapons and cameras. Thereupon, his men made their search with that same colossal air of detachment that Stefan had sensed in them from afar, that same self-assurance.

What on earth breed of creature was this, anyway? Stefan asked himself this question as he watched the soldier casually go through his pack and search under his mattress. Absurdly enough, the whole mystery seemed to lie in that easy chewing of the cud.

"What are they chewing, anyway?" Stefan whispered to Koval, who stood watching.

Koval shook his head. "Tobacco maybe?" he suggested.

Stefan followed the soldier out into the hall where

his officer stood, surrounded by a group of the refugees. "And what's to become of us?" one of them asked.

"The relocation of refugees is the concern of the proper authorities, madam," the officer replied.

"But we will have our say about it, surely?" the woman asked, anxiously.

There was anxiety on the other faces, too, as everyone waited for the answer.

"There's nothing to worry about, madam."

Anxiety gave way to puzzlement. Not worry? Mr. Behun voiced their concern. "We have all lived through too much, sir," he said, "and suffered at the hands of too many to take the word of anyone that we are not to worry."

The soldier only shrugged his shoulders, then turned on his heel and led his squad out of the schoolhouse. Out in the yard, where the children had gathered, they stopped to distribute chocolate bars and something called "gum." Even Stefan, who had followed them out, got some of each.

Like the others, he ate the chocolate at once. It was pure chocolate, too, with not even a suspicion of fake stuff. Tasting it on his tongue was pure bliss.

As for the gum, however, none of them knew what to do with it. Each stick was hardly two bites. But a grown-up who knew English and had read the label said, "It's goom . . . something to chew. Try it."

So for the rest of the afternoon most of them went about with jaws working incessantly, as long as the gum lasted. "Okh," one of the women cried, laughing, "they look like so many calves! I'll be glad when that goom's all gone!"

"Ah, well, in the meantime, let them enjoy themselves for once. They're children. . . ."

So far, then, the Americans turned out to be not so bad as they had always been painted at home. But only a few years before, the Germans, too, had been greeted as saviors by most of the populace at home. Yet not many weeks had passed before they were suffering the same dispossession, the same murder and enserfment as they had suffered at the hands of the Soviets.

So watch out. They're mild enough now, these Americans. But wait . . . just wait. So Stefan, feeling unusually wise, told himself.

fifteen

For Stefan and the others, the coming of the Americans in some ways meant an immediate turn for the better. For one thing, the hounding from place to place ceased altogether. By official military order, they were to stay where they were for the time being; for another, their hunger began to ease.

Even though the Germans were themselves short of supply that spring, the Americans now ordered them to issue more generous food rations to the refugees. Stefan, too, received a new ration card, without even asking for it. And, one day, everyone in the schoolhouse was issued a loaf of bread from the American commissary.

Mothers called to their children. "Come, little doves, eat!"

Back in his corner with his loaf, Stefan undid the waxpaper wrapping and found the bread already sliced, each slice precisely the same as the last. With a delicious feeling of luxury he selected one, but before taking a bite he turned it over several times. It was as white as snow.

"Tasteless," old man Kostur remarked, just as Stefan was taking his first bite.

"That's because they've left out the straw, my friend," Mr. Behun replied. "You've got used to eating straw, so now you crave it. For you they'll have to bake special bread."

Having wolfed three slices of the bread, one right after another, Stefan lay back on his mattress and pondered the gift. He could not understand these people, the Americans. Surely they had no hope that their kindnesses would ever be repaid? Yet here they were handing out such generous gifts—and without even being asked!

But despite the gift of bread, in the schoolhouse new fearful questions were being asked. At night, before he fell asleep, Stefan lay listening to the talk among the men in his corner. The topic was almost always the same: what will we do if the Soviets break into our region of refuge? Before this dreaded possibility, all other concerns were swept away.

In front of Berlin, the Soviet Army is locked in a death struggle with units of the Wehrmacht and the Home Guard who are defending the German capital and Hitler in his underground hideaway. Berlin's about to fall. Why, then, they asked, is the American Eisenhower holding back? He could have taken Berlin himself, weeks ago. But now his troops are suddenly halted on the Elbe, only two days from Berlin. And farther south, too, the Americans seem suddenly reined back, as if by some mysterious hand.

No, brothers, something here smells.

"Ye-e-s. And then they could even let the Soviets in on purpose." There. From his corner Koval had said it.

A moment's silence, then: "They won't get me again. I'll fight till I drop," someone said.

"With bare hands?"

At last one morning early in May came the news over the radio: Berlin has fallen and Germany has capitulated.

Stefan had never pictured to himself how the war would end, how it would feel for it to end, and peace to begin. This war had been going on altogether for nearly half of his life—six of his fourteen years—and by now he remembered peace only in fragments.

For those in the schoolhouse, the war's end was something of an anticlimax. Stefan himself was surprised to realize that all along he had been thinking of the coming of the Americans to the town a few days before as having marked the war's end. But now it was really over. Over at last . . . at long last.

That was a Sunday. For most of those in the schoolhouse, it was Orthodox Easter as well, the most important holiday of the year. But that cold and rainy Easter of 1945 came and went almost entirely unmarked in the schoolhouse.

Instead, people gathered in groups and talked quietly, soberly of what lay ahead for refugees such as themselves. Restless, impatient of being confined indoors by the heavy rain, Stefan wandered aimlessly from room to room wishing for someone his own age to talk to. Martin? Even him. . . .

"Because you may be sure," Koval was saying, "that they're already settling their accounts with our people at home—taking their vengeance. And our people unarmed. . . ."

"Ah, yes . . . and what's to become of us here?" old man Kostur asked. "And what about this boy?" he added, nodding toward Stefan. "What of him? Father gone. . . . What's he to do?"

"I can go home," Stefan spoke up. "Everything will be taken care of, once I get there."

Everything. He'd go to whichever school they sent him, study whatever they assigned him. And afterward. . . . He took a deep breath. Afterward, he'd go wherever they told him to, work at whatever was assigned to him.

Mr. Behun gave a short laugh. "Everything!" he repeated Stefan's word. "But if I know your father, my boy. . . ." He broke off. "Now that was a man," he said, turning toward old man Kostur.

Stefan listened intently, waiting for more.

"He was in a penal squad, you know," Mr. Behun went on. "How he survived, God alone knows. Many's the time, he told me, he was just a jelly of fear inside. But he never let it possess him. He believed in his

137

own future. Maybe that's what saw him through. And with no bravado, mind you. No chest-thumping on his part."

Stefan threw himself back down on his mattress and, for the first time, allowed his thoughts to dwell upon his father. What Mr. Behun had said was that, in his unspectacular way, his father had been a man of courage. To Stefan's surprise, now that the idea had been expressed, it seemed to fit. He thought back. Yes, just as Mr. Behun had said, there hadn't been any bravado, any chest-thumping.

But that must be the very thing that had made his father seem, on the whole, such an ordinary man. Maybe that's why he had not realized—till he had heard it from another—what his father truly was. He wondered: did his father have to die for him to learn what sort of man he was?

Stefan sighed. None of his father's resourcefulness, none of his purpose, none of his belief in the future had rubbed off on him. Well, it didn't matter much now. At home he would need none of these. He would not need to strive to save himself, the way his father had. . . .

Then, feeling restless, he got up and, seeing that the rain had stopped at last, went out. He wandered about the schoolyard for a time, threading his way around the puddles, and then, with nothing better to do, took off for town.

As usual these days, the streets were full of army trucks and jeeps speeding by. Stefan loitered at shop windows for a time but, at last, still restless, he turned his steps back toward the schoolhouse.

Then he saw it. A jeep, driven by an American sergeant—but with a Russian colonel as passenger. Stefan stood for a moment, not believing his eyes. So the Soviets really had come, were already here, just as the concentration camp survivor had threatened—just as those in the schoolhouse had feared.

Stefan broke into a run after the jeep. It had been stopped by a military policeman directing traffic, but just as Stefan came running up, it started on again. All the same, he had a good look. That, in truth, was a Russian colonel seated grand as you please in the American jeep.

Stefan turned about and raced all the way back to the schoolhouse.

sixteen

"BUT ARE YOU SURE YOU ACTUALLY SAW ONE?"

Stefan stood surrounded by the crowd bombarding him with questions about the frightful news he had brought to the schoolhouse.

"What was he wearing? . . . What color was his uniform? . . . What insignia?"

As if he didn't know a Red Army colonel when he saw one!

"It's clear, then, they've come to a secret understanding of some sort," Mr. Behun said at last. "They've conquered Germany, so now they're preparing to divide it up among themselves."

"But which part will go to the Soviets?" Koval asked. "That's the burning question!"

At length, that same day, a committee of five who spoke good English was chosen and dispatched to the American Command in town to find out what they could about an understanding between the Americans and the Soviets, to find out the meaning of the presence of a Red Army man in this town that had been conquered by the Americans. Mr. Behun, one of the committee, was chosen as its spokesman.

They left, and were back within the hour. "The first thing they asked us," Mr. Behun reported, "was, 'Why don't you people want to go home? Everyone else is going home—the Poles, the French, the Dutch. . . .' "

He spread his hands in a gesture of helplessness. "Before such abyssmal innocence, where to begin? As for the existence of an understanding, they said, 'We can't say anything officially . . . but we'll give you a week's notice.' "

"So that means . . ."

"That means," Mr. Behun interjected, "that our guess is true. They're going to divide Germany into zones."

"But which will be the American zone? That's the main question," Koval put in, "for we have to be in the American zone."

"Who doesn't? But they would not say. Only that we will have a week's notice."

After that day, a sharp eye was kept on the comings and goings of the military command and reported at once in the schoolhouse. For lack of any official information, every least move caused a fresh wave of fearful rumors among them.

More than anything else, that first glimpse of the Red Army man and the electric reaction of his fellow refugees pushed Stefan further out of his prolonged lethargy. More and more frequently now, he spent his days wandering about the town. And he saw more than one Red Army man riding about in jeeps and walking the streets.

American soldiers were everywhere. Stefan longed for some more of the chocolate they were continually handing out. But he was ashamed to join the children who swarmed around them.

By now he had learned most of the insignia and could tell sergeants from corporals and lieutenants from captains. American military police were about, too, but whenever Stefan spied one he ducked out of sight at once. Though he was careful always to carry his papers in his pocket, best not to risk being confronted by this new, unknown, and untried authority.

O.K. Okay.

Stefan heard that word frequently now, but he still wasn't sure of its meaning. It probably meant "good-by" because it was often uttered with a wave of the hand, whereupon departure followed.

In the schoolhouse, as the rumors grew, the poison of new fear embittered the lives of the refugees. One day early in June, Koval himself came back from town with the most disturbing report yet. "Those Reds roving about in American jeeps," he said, "are actually hunting down refugees. They're shipping them in carloads back to the Soviet Union. Not only from here, but from all over Germany. So be careful, friends. . . ."

The very next day, this soul-chilling report seemed

to be confirmed by some news brought to the school-house by none other than Mr. Volodko. He appeared at the schoolhouse early that morning. "But only for overnight," he told Mr. Behun.

It seemed that he was on his way to Hesse, the neighboring region, where his committee was to meet with the American Command. "The Americans," he said, "are setting up refugee camps there. But we want to establish our own camp for our own people. And so we must get their permission and then search for a place."

"Make it as far westward as possible," Koval instructed him. "Just in case. . . ."

And then Mr. Volodko told them that only the week before in some place in Austria, the English had forcibly handed over to the Soviets thousands of refugees for repatriation. "There was even a pitched battle," he said, "and many died. Many drowned themselves in the river rather than go."

Out of the shocked silence, old man Kostur finally spoke. "There are thousands of us here, too, don't forget. So . . ."

"We figure two million of us Ukrainians alone," Mr. Volodko interrupted, "counting refugees, forced laborers, and concentration camp inmates."

"There you are! Two million," Mr. Kostur repeated. "So if we all stick together, here in Germany it won't be so easy for them to hand us over."

"No, we'll fight!" Koval exclaimed. "So long as we breathe, we'll fight!"

"Aha! Now that's good cossack talk!" Mr. Volodko

said. "That's the kind of talk I like to hear! So I say, brothers and sisters, that we must hold together as one. Come what may, together as one! That way they won't be able to pluck us off. . . ."

Afterward, that evening, Mr. Volodko sat with Stefan in a quiet corner and talked. He put his arm around Stefan's shoulder. "I heard about your father, Stefko," he said.

Stefan sat mute, staring straight ahead.

"There was a man!" Mr. Volodko continued. "And even though he's gone, Stefko, he'll see you through. Somehow, he'll see you through."

Stefan did not know what Mr. Volodko meant by this but, strangely, the words gave him a measure of comfort.

"Just take good care of that valise of his," Mr. Volodko continued. "Something will come of it some day."

Stefan did not have the courage to confess that he had not yet gone for the valise; that, so far as he knew, it still reposed in that stable where his father had stowed it.

Early next morning, Mr. Volodko was again on his way to Hesse.

The refugees continued to live as if on an active volcano, ready to flee at the first sign of a Soviet take-over. Where? Which direction? No one knew.

As for Stefan, during those days of terrible uncertainty, he found himself thinking more and more of home. Once again, after all these many months and all that had happened to him, he could at will imagine himself going up the stairs, two at a time, to their flat on the third floor, the way he used to do. Only, when he got to their door and turned the knob, there'd be nobody there.

Where would he go? Who would take him in? Not Pavlo and his family. They were tight for space, as it was. Besides, by now maybe Pavlo had someone else for a best friend. . . .

He could not make himself enter the flat. In his thoughts, he turned away from that door without opening it. All the same, unbidden, thoughts of home continued to crowd his dreams, and he did not try to banish them.

And then, one morning, an American sergeant came and affixed a notice on the wall beside the front door. At once people came out of the classrooms to read what was typed in several Slavic languages: "Attention! An important meeting will be held today at 1300 hours in the hall of this building. All are requested to attend."

"Imagine," Koval murmured, turning away, " 'requested'. . . ."

The news spread throughout the schoolhouse with the speed of light. At last. At long last, official word was forthcoming. Hope grew and the pall of gloom that had oppressed the refugees began to lift.

As the hour of one approached, Stefan joined the crowd gathering in the hall. It was already full when he entered and a murmur of talk filled the room.

Almost precisely at the appointed hour, the front

door opened and an American lieutenant stepped in. But on his heels who should follow but a man in Red Army uniform. A colonel, no less.

For a moment, stunned silence. Then a pandemonium of derisive shouts, whistles, stamping of feet, and catcalls.

Through it all, the colonel gazed at them impassively, as if he heard nothing. The American lieutenant, surprise plain on his face, stood waiting. At last, he held up his hand for silence. The furor subsided at once.

Then, at a nod from him, the Red Army colonel stepped forward and began to speak in Russian. "Brothers and sisters!" he shouted, as if making a speech to a vast throng outdoors.

At this the uproar exploded all over again, all but lifting the roof off the schoolhouse.

"Who're you calling brothers and sisters, you dog's son?"

"Back into your hole, vermin!"

"Don't come sniffing round decent people!"

The American lieutenant held up his hand again. "Wait! Hear him out!" he shouted in German.

Shouts of "Let him speak!" came from various parts of the hall. The crowd quieted and the colonel began again. This time he spoke in a heavily accented Ukrainian, with many mistakes in pronunciation. "I've been sent by the families you left behind to beg you to come home," he said. "Everything will be forgiven you!"

"What gall!"

"Forgive what, you dog's son!"

"And who's to forgive that pal of yours in Moscow?"

Unperturbed, the man paused, then went on. "Your families are waiting for you! Your homes await you! Your native land awaits you!"

" 'Siberia awaits you!' " someone mocked.

But the colonel only paused for the laughter to die down before continuing. "Why wander among strangers when your brothers and sisters all await you with open arms?" Here in a theatrical gesture, he spread wide his arms.

"Okh!" a woman's voice cried out. "Just look! He's even been to drama school!"

Laughter burst out all over the hall. Stefan, leaning against the wall, laughed too.

The colonel dropped his arms and stood gazing out at them—his eyes round and innocent—and this only fed their laughter. Then someone at the back of the hall opened the door into one of the classrooms and disappeared through it, still laughing. Others followed his example, dispersing in all directions. In another five minutes, the hall was empty.

Stefan sat on his mattress and listened to the talk of his roommates.

"But it's no laughing matter, brothers!" old man Kostur said. "We're caught in a bear's den, blindfolded."

"Well, at least now we know which way the wind blows," Mr. Behun said.

"It blows cold. . . ."

147

seventeen

NOT UNTIL THE FIFTEENTH OF JUNE DID WORD COME to the schoolhouse, and throughout Germany and the world as well: all of East Germany, Thuringia included, had been awarded to the Soviets as their zone. Takeover was scheduled for 500 hours on June 22. All those wishing to leave. . . .

Wishing to leave!

Within the hour, the schoolhouse inhabitants were in a fever of packing and making preparations for an early morning departure. Most were planning to flee southward, into Bavaria, others westward to Hesse where the Ukrainian Committee had established one of several camps for their own people.

That same afternoon, a jeep pulled up in front of the schoolhouse and two Americans got out, a corporal and a lieutenant. By the time they entered, nearly all those within were already awaiting them in the hall. To their astonishment, the lieutenant greeted them in Ukrainian. "Good day, good people. I have been ordered to come here today to make an announcement."

"Are you an American . . . or what?" someone asked.

"I am," the lieutenant said, smiling. "But my parents are Ukrainian, born in Ukraine and emigrated to the United States before the first World War. I learned Ukrainian from them."

"It's not bad. Not bad at all!"

"I've come," the lieutenant went on, "to tell you that temporary camps have been established in the American zone for displaced persons and . . ."

"Displaced persons? What's that?"

"That's the name for refugees," the lieutenant replied. "The nearest such camp is just over the border, only a few kilometers away, in the Hesse region. Many of your countrymen are already there. Our people are waiting there to help you. Daily rations will be provided everyone. All who wish to go to the American zone have only to apply to me at the command post and I will issue your pass."

"But what about those such as I?" Mr. Behun spoke up. He held up his cane. "As you see . . ."

"I'll try to find transport for all who are unable to go on foot," the lieutenant replied.

"And what about this boy?" Mr. Behun asked, pointing to Stefan. "We're traveling together."

149

"Then you'll go together," the lieutenant said.

He answered a few more questions, made a few more remarks and then, with a smile and a wave of the hand, left, followed by the corporal. The moment the front door slammed shut, the room burst alive with voices, all talking at once.

" 'Displaced persons'!" Koval exclaimed. "Tell me, what kind of mealy-mouthed talk is that? I was hounded out of my homeland! Pushed and shoved. Thieves and murderers displaced me!"

"Sh. Sh.," some woman tried to quiet him. "The man was only trying to do his duty. He's not responsible for what others did."

"But you heard what he said, that passes will be issued. . . ."

"So what?" Koval retorted. "Once, just once, I'd like to come and go like a man, without pass, passport, paper, or document. Just once!"

Mr. Behun laughed. "You're dreaming, my friend."

"Something about it smells. They're going to get us all into a heap and then . . ."

Stefan, leaning against the wall, listened to this talk. Without even consulting him, Mr. Behun had assumed that he would go along with him. Well, he assumed too much! When Stefan returned to his pallet, he found old man Kostur packing. "Where are you going, Grandad? Bavaria or Hesse?"

The old man straightened. "I think we should go to Hesse, my son. It's closer. And there'll be food in the American camp."

150

Somehow, the old man's "we" was more acceptable than Mr. Behun's. Stefan's defiance melted away. For now at least he'd go wherever the wind carried him. That was less bothersome than deciding for himself.

True to the lieutenant's promise, the next day at precisely the appointed hour, a truck appeared in front of the schoolhouse. "That's the American way of doing things," Mr. Behun explained. "They say that time is money."

The truck, a large open one, driven by a private accompanied by the same corporal, looked brand new. The soldiers helped them to load their baggage, then helped the women and children and old people onto the truck. It was so roomy that they could sit, if they chose. Within fifteen minutes, all their baggage was stowed.

The soldiers climbed into the cab of the truck and they were off. There was no one to see them off, for the schoolhouse was empty. Those who were going on foot had started out at daybreak.

Stefan stood and gazed back at the schoolhouse as it receded into the distance, into the past. No one spoke. It was as if each were saying his own final, silent good-by to yet another episode in his broken life.

Then . . . the valise. Only now did he remember the valise. He had forgotten to go after it. Yes, forgotten, he told himself in angry defiance, tears suddenly in his eyes. Plant a cross . . . plant a cross . . .

plant a cross. . . . The phrase pounded in his head in rhythm with the motion of the truck.

The road was alive with crowds of refugees like themselves, all hastening to get out of Thuringia before the fatal day and hour. Fear on every face. Their worldly goods on their backs, they hurried along as fast as they could, looking neither to the right nor the left. Most were on foot. The lucky ones, like themselves, were traveling by horse and wagon or by motor vehicle. It was like the war all over again, except that now they were not under menace of bomb or gunfire. Overhead, the brilliant sky was already darkening, but toward the west it was still bright with sunshine, as if it were a signal of some promised land well beyond human reach.

Then, as Stefan stood gazing ahead, he saw that for some reason the refugees on foot were ducking into the forest along either side, leaving the road empty for a unit of uniformed men marching along behind them, carbines on their backs. He stared. He'd know that uniform anywhere.

There was a stir on either side of him. "Soviets!" someone muttered. "What the devil are they doing here?"

"They must be on their way to man the border," Mr. Behun said.

"What border?" Stefan asked.

"Why, of Thuringia, my boy. Once we leave this region, we'll not be able to get back in."

"Who'd want to?" a voice behind them spoke up.

By now their truck was overtaking the marching men, and as they drew abreast, faces turned and they eyed each other. Stefan sensed a curious, impassable gulf between themselves in their truck, a little moving island of another world, and the marching men.

"Poor devils . . ." someone murmured.

Then someone began a song, under his breath, as if to himself. Another voice took up the tune. Then another and another, until soon almost a dozen voices were singing, unrolling a ribbon of song behind them as they sped along the highway. But it was a sad song and when it was done, a brooding silence fell upon them and they did not sing again.

After a while, old man Kostur, standing beside Stefan, began a running commentary on the passing landscape. "Look," he said, as they came around a turn. "Look at that mill! Not like those at home. And what's that stone statue standing in front of it?"

"It's a gnome," Mr. Behun said.

"Imagine!" The old man shook his head in surprise. "With us at home, not gnomes but devils inhabit mills. You don't believe it? Hoo! The stories I could tell you about that!"

"We're over the border in Hesse now," Mr. Behun said at last. He took a deep breath. "Safe."

They crossed a river. A few minutes later they were approaching a large complex of brick buildings and slowing down. This must be it.

The truck came to a halt at the gate. And now, suddenly, Stefan saw the fence—a high fence of steel mesh, rows of barbed wire strung along the top. At the gate, an armed American soldier stood guard.

"I don't like barbed wire fences," Mr. Behun said loudly. "No way do I like barbed wire fences."

A woman's voice suddenly screamed out. "No! No! We won't go! We won't go!"

Other voices arose, screaming and shouting.

Within the compound of the camp, children paused in their games, people stood and stared, then came running to the fence. The guard at the gate had come to attention.

By now the people in the truck were shouting to the skies, to whomever would listen . . . to the deaf world. Stefan heard himself shouting along with the rest. At the same time, some of the men were frantically trying to unfasten the tail gate.

The young corporal who had accompanied them appeared beside the truck, shouting, too, and holding up a hand for silence. But the screaming continued. Children were wailing, "Mama! Ma-ma-a-a!"

The sound sent a chill down Stefan's back.

By now the other side of the fence was lined with spectators. At last, as suddenly as it had begun, the screaming stopped. The corporal stood looking up at them, bewilderment on his face. "But this is only a camp for displaced persons," he began, speaking in English. "Only until we find out where everyone's going. Meantime, you'll get good food, shelter . . ."

"It's a trick! We know such tricks! We were nurtured on them at home."

The corporal stood uncertain for a moment. "When we have everyone all together," he began again, "we'll know how to help. Now . . ."

"Just as I said! They're gathering us all into a heap, then they'll summon their precious allies, and say, 'Here they are, comrades! All yours!' "

"Listen, it's no trick," the corporal repeated.

"Then what's the fence for? And the guard?"

"Just to keep order. Nothing more."

"Wait a minute, my friends," someone broke in. It was Mr. Behun. "We don't need to risk it. There's that other camp, the one that our own committee was to establish. Where is it?" he asked the corporal. "It must be nearby."

The Americans, now apparently weary of the affair as a bad business, consented to take them to the other camp. "Only you'll be sorry," the corporal told them, as he climbed back into the truck. "This D.P. camp provides food, whereas in the other . . ." He did not finish.

In less than ten minutes, they were at the other camp. It, too, was fenced in, also with barbed wire. A guard stood at the gate here, too. But above the camp waved a flag of blue and gold. Stefan caught his breath when he saw it. It was the Ukrainian flag. At home it was worth one's very life even to display its colors, let alone fly it."

"This is more like it!" old man Kostur said, as he jumped stiffly down off the truck.

Within the compound, to one side of the low buildings, towered a tall brick smokestack. Crowds of people could be seen moving among the buildings. In one part of the large yard, among bare mounds of yellow dirt, some children were playing. Near them a bunch of boys were kicking a ball around. Stefan strained his eyes as he waited his turn to get down off the truck. But he saw no familiar faces.

eighteen

THE CAMP HAD ONCE BEEN A BRICKWORKS. THOUGH the buildings were substantial enough, they were dirty and cheerless. In an effort to achieve some sort of privacy in the big, barn-like buildings, people had strung up blankets, clothing, even rags to make little individual cubicles. There were no tables and only a few stools. As for beds, people slept on pallets, on cots, in bunks—whatever they had been able to acquire. For covers they used their own clothes.

After wandering up and down among the cubicles, Stefan, Mr. Behun, and old man Kostur found an unoccupied triple tier of bunks in a far corner. It had apparently been hastily and inexpertly knocked together with scrap boards, for it swayed visibly as Stefan climbed up to the top bunk. That probably explained why it had remained unclaimed till now.

Stowing his pack, Stefan fumbled about in his

coat pocket and found half of a precious potato that he had saved from the day before, carefully wrapped in a bit of newspaper. He hadn't eaten yet that day and he was hungry. The potato, though cold, tasted delicious.

That night Stefan slept hardly at all, for even during the middle of the night the whole barracks was astir with the continuous arrival of new people fleeing the Soviet zone. Whenever he awakened, he lay listening for a familiar voice. But he heard none.

In the days that followed, crowds of refugees continued to stream into the brickworks. Within three days, the camp grew from some two hundred people to an anthill of well over a thousand. It grew so crowded that finally the latest comers, using any material they could lay their hands on to mark off separate compartments, were forced to pitch camp outdoors, around the tall smokestack in the middle of the compound.

One day soon after his own arrival, as Stefan was passing by the dens clustered around the smokestack, he heard a woman's voice call his name. At first he did not turn around, for how many Stefans were there among the hundreds that were milling about the compound? Dozens and dozens, probably, and strangers to him all.

But on the second call he did turn. And there stood Dr. Olha. Of all people, Dr. Olha. He ran up to her and, to his own surprise, by way of greeting he flung his arms around her. Her embrace was as warm as his.

When Dr. Olha learned that Mr. Behun was also in the camp, she insisted upon looking him up at once. The three of them held a reunion.

"But where are the Stefanyks and Granny Sophia?" Not Stefan, but Mr. Behun asked the question.

"I met them weeks and weeks ago, during my wanderings," Dr. Olha replied. "Mrs. Natalia was especially upset over having become separated from you three. After that, I myself lost track of them, for to find shelter we had to separate." Dr. Olha turned toward Stefan. "I heard about your father, Stefan. I hope you are taking good care of that valise of his, because . . ."

She must have seen the dismay on Stefan's face, for she stopped. After that, feeling Mr. Behun's look of censure on his back, Stefan made his escape as soon as he could. He had forgotten the valise and that was an end of it, he told himself.

With the last of his cigarettes in his pocket, he set forth for the nearby town to find something to eat. He would stay and explore it, too, he decided, if only to keep out of sight of Dr. Olha and Mr. Behun.

Guided by a tall Gothic tower on the near horizon, Stefan soon found himself in a church square in the very center of town. A market place was spread in the shadow of the church. Going from stall to stall, he began to look for something he could afford. But he had to wander about the market for a long time before he found it: a piece of yellow cheese and a bun for only six cigarettes.

159

He counted his remaining supply—only eight. What would he do when these were gone? Many of the refugees, he knew, had taken to collecting the butts of only partly smoked cigarettes thrown away by the wasteful Americans. I'll do that, too, Stefan decided.

Munching the bread and cheese, he left the market place and strolled up one of the narrow streets that led from the little square like the spokes of a wheel. The town was crowded with American soldiers, most of them riding about in jeeps. Stefan, however, no longer stared at them as he had at first.

Now he came upon a row of little shops. Here, at last, was something to look at, a pleasant way to spend his time. Though he had not a mark in his pocket, it didn't matter. Still eating, he stopped to linger in front of one after the other! An apothecary, a cobbler, a green grocer . . .

A music shop.

The dusty window was filled with a variety of small musical instruments—a flute, a horn, several harmonicas. But in the very center, upon a faded pink cloth artfully folded into little hills and valleys, rested an accordion.

As if he had come upon a ghost, Stefan stopped and stared, the last of the bread and cheese forgotten in his hand. A rush of memories came crowding in upon him. Music lessons on Saturdays in the Pioneer Palace, humming with the activities of his school friends. Soccer games with a real soccer ball. Exploring along the river with Pavlo and the others—

always Pavlo. His mother's pleasure whenever he played a new piece for her on the accordion. . . .

Someone was standing beside him. Aware of this, Stefan nevertheless kept his eyes fixed upon the accordion. Then a pleasant voice—a Russian voice—spoke. "You play, isn't that true? But you had to leave yours behind."

Stefan looked up. Beside him stood a man in Red Army uniform, a captain. He had a broad grin on his face and his eyebrows were raised in mock surprise, as if he were prompting Stefan.

For a long moment, Stefan stared up at him. Then, without a word, he turned on his heel and broke into a run. As he ran, he felt an impulse to look back and see what effect his sudden, wordless departure had had on the man. But he managed to refrain.

nineteen

STEFAN TOOK CARE NOT TO MENTION THE SOVIET captain to any of the inhabitants of the brickworks. The news that Soviets had somehow gained entry, even into their new refuge, would have caused fresh alarm. Anyway, it was not the Soviet captain that stuck in his thoughts, but the accordion in the shop window. It kept tugging at him and the feeling was pleasant.

He could almost feel it in his hands, feel the weight of it on his shoulders and arms. In the relative privacy of his bunk he moved his fingers and arm as if he were playing one of the pieces he knew. Doing this, he could even hear the music in his head. Now how about "The Blue Danube"? That was his mother's favorite.

If only he had an accordion, it would help. He wouldn't need anyone. If he had an accordion. After all, hadn't his father promised him one? He must have known!

Stefan began to turn over in his mind how he might acquire the accordion in the window. He was nearly out of cigarettes. But what about butts? How many would they ask for the accordion? Almost at once, he discarded this idea as absurd. As soon try to buy diamonds with cigarette butts!

He still had the soap . . . but that he would never give up. Not for anything. No, not even for an accordion.

But at least he could look at the accordion all he pleased. So the next day he went to town again and searched out the musical instrument shop.

The window had not been disturbed since the day before. Perhaps it had not been touched throughout the entire war. Stefan loitered at the shop window for an hour or so, then returned to the brickworks.

When he reached there, he found it in a state of near panic. For someone had spied a Soviet Army officer in the town and had brought back the alarming news.

Wild rumors were born again and grew with each telling. The nearby American Army camp was said to be shared by a picked squad of Red Army men, and these were prowling the streets on the hunt for refugees. They were collecting the helpless victims of these manhunts in the camp until they had enough for a carload.

All sorts of other scum prowled the streets of the town, it was said. Intriguers. Stool pigeons. Stay away from the town, the word went around. Or, if you must risk it for some overriding purpose, the minute you see one of these manhunters, run. Run for your very life. . . .

Now, almost daily, a small delegation—each time a different one, in case this should help—was dispatched to the American Command to discover, if possible, what was their true policy, so the refugees might learn what lay in store for them. In vain. Smiles. Soft words. Denials.

Fear stalked the brickworks.

But Stefan hardly felt any of this turmoil. Nor did he pay any attention to the urging of both Dr. Olha and Mr. Behun that he join the classes that had been organized for school-aged children. He was on his own and could do as he pleased. So nearly every day, rain or shine, he set forth for the town. As soon as he was out of sight of the brickworks, he broke into a run and ran all the way to the musical instrument shop.

One day, as he stood in front of the window staring at "his" accordion, it occurred to him that he might go inside and ask to try it, as if he had thoughts of buying it. He gazed speculatively at the door, a blank slab of wood. He had never seen anyone go in or out of it.

Come on, try it! What's there to lose? It's probably locked anyway.

Stefan walked over to it and stood gathering courage. At long last, he pressed down the latch and pushed. To his surprise, the door opened. A woman stood inside. She turned toward him, a smile on her face.

His courage vanished. "Oh!" he blurted, stepping back. "Mistake . . . excuse me!"

He shut the door with a bang and fled headlong down the street. Looking back once as he ran, he saw the woman standing on the sidewalk now, her arms akimbo, staring in his direction.

He ducked down a side street and ran till he had reached the edge of town. As he approached a large group of buildings surrounded by a fence, he slowed at last to a walk. Jeeps were passing back and forth through the gate where an American soldier stood, rifle in hand. So this must be the American Army camp.

Keeping a wary eye on the guard, Stefan began to skirt the fence that surrounded the camp. The guard paid no attention, or perhaps he did not even see him. Stefan continued to follow the fence. At one place, he stopped for a while to watch a ball game of some sort, played with a club. Then he went on.

When, at last, he had worked his way halfway around the camp, there at the back, outside an open gate, he came upon an enormous pile of large brown tin cans, bottles, and cartons thrown in a heap. At first, he didn't know what to make of it. But while he was crouching there behind some bushes, eyeing the pile, a soldier with his shirt sleeves rolled up, came out of the gate carrying a large can. He tossed it

165

toward the top of the heap. It fell with a clatter and rolled down to the bottom. Unconcerned, the soldier went back inside.

Stefan waited. He looked all around. No one in sight. Cautiously, he crept forward. When he reached the pile and saw what it was, he stood for a moment, dumbfounded. It was a garbage dump.

But what a garbage dump!

He picked up a big can, similar to the one the soldier had just tossed out, and looked within. Something lay at the bottom. He thrust in his hand, dipped a finger into the stuff, then drew it out again. He couldn't believe his eyes. Strawberry jam! He licked it off his finger.

Carefully he set that can aside, picked up another, and peered inside. Almost a cupful of something left in this one. He stuck in a finger and licked it. Peach! He picked up yet another tin, this one a square oblong one. In it he found two cookies still left in the box. These he took out and thrust into his pocket.

Stefan had sometimes had dreams of finding money. The dream was nearly always the same. He'd be walking along when, suddenly, lying strewn at his feet were coins. Elated, he began picking them up. But the more and the faster he picked, the more coins there were. Always, unfortunately, he woke before he had succeeded in gathering them all. And always, of course, though a little to his surprise—so vivid had been the dream—he awoke empty-handed.

Going around that kitchen dump, picking up can after can and peering within, Stefan felt he was reliving that dream. But this time it was real.

Suddenly, as he was rooting about in the dump, a heavy hand dropped onto his shoulder. The hand turned him firmly about and there stood the soldier with sleeves rolled up.

"You hungry?" the man said in English. "Come on!"

And, without letting go his grip, he marched Stefan through the gate and into a building that turned out to be the camp kitchen. It was a huge room, full of stoves and great shining pots. Several soldiers now surrounded him. They talked rapidly among themselves for a few moments. Then his captor led him to a small table in a corner of the room and sat him down. "Stay here!" he ordered, pointing a finger at him.

He left, but in a few moments returned with a tray heaped with food. He set it down in front of Stefan. "Okay?" He smiled.

Bewildered by this turn of events, Stefan did not know what to answer. The soldier indicated the tray. "Eat!" he said.

Stefan fell to. While he ate, the men kept talking to him, first in English, and then in scraps of broken German. Stefan could only look at them. He did not know how to answer. At last, his captor said "okay" again and left.

Stefan ate on. He couldn't remember when he had

had such a feast. Chicken. A mountain of snow-white mashed potatoes with a big golden lake of melted butter on top. Green peas. Milk, a big glass of it. And a big piece of pastry with sliced apples inside. In a word, a banquet.

He was just finishing the pastry when his captor came back. With him was another man in uniform.

Stefan leaped to his feet with such suddenness that his chair fell back with a clatter. For this one wore a Red Army uniform. A captain. As Stefan, his heart pounding like a sledge hammer against the wall of his chest, looked up at him, recognition passed between them. It was the same man who had spoken to him in front of the music shop.

The man laughed. "I'm not going to eat you! Still dreaming of that accordion?" Without waiting for an answer he went on, speaking now in Ukrainian. "Why torture yourself? We've got accordions to burn in our quarters here in camp . . . and no one to play them properly."

Stefan could hardly speak for the pounding of his heart. "I haven't . . . played for a long time," he finally said.

"That doesn't matter. One never forgets a thing like that. You'd be doing us a favor."

Stefan stood silent, his thoughts in confusion. It sounded more like an invitation than an order. Was he their prisoner or not? He stole a look at his American captor, but he couldn't tell.

"Come on! What are you afraid of?"

"I'm not afraid," Stefan lied.

"I'll tell you what," the Russian said. "You wait here a minute."

With that he disappeared. But in less than three minutes he was back, not only with an accordion in his arms, but with three or four of his comrades as well. He thrust the instrument at Stefan. "Here! Play us a tune!"

Stefan took it. He hefted it in his arms. And then he looked up and grinned broadly at them all.

"Play us a tune!" one of the men urged.

Stefan gave the accordion a tentative squeeze. A wheezy note came out. Frowning, he looked it over. "Oh. Here's a place in the bellows that's worn through. See?"

"Listen, you," the captain said in a take-it-or-leave-it tone, "that thing's been through fire and brimstone! But you ought to be able to squeeze something out of it!"

"But you said . . ."

"That we've got accordions to burn?" He laughed and his eyebrows shot up. "As for that, we've already burned them!"

Stefan, too, had to laugh at the joke, along with the others. He experimented for a few minutes and found that, if he just ignored the wheeze, he could get passable music out of the instrument after all. Hearing the sound, men began drifting toward them until he had a sizeable audience around him.

He swung into a polka. A chorus of approval from the men when he'd finished. He played another.

"The kid's not bad . . . not half bad. . . . Play

169

some more! D'you know this one?" And someone whistled a fragment of a tune until Stefan picked it up and continued it.

Gradually, while he played, Stefan felt the last of the wall of isolation, behind which he had lived ever since his father's death, falling away. He smiled around at his audience. As if by magic, he was a part of his surroundings again, a part of the world.

But it was already getting dark. Stefan looked up at the Russian captain, whom the men called Igor. "I have to go now," he said.

But it was more a question than a statement. He didn't yet know whether he was free to go. Maybe the American soldier really did consider him his prisoner?

The Russian captain waved a hand. "Sure. Go ahead!" he said.

Stefan slipped the straps off his shoulders and laid the accordion down on the table—but slowly, regretfully, all the while praying passionately, almost aloud, that the captain would say, "Oh, take it along. It's yours!"

It was, after all, a poor instrument, and defective besides. On the other hand, not since the day he had left home, all those miles ago, had he got so close to having an accordion . . . the one his father had promised him. But all Captain Igor said was, "Come back tomorrow! Come back any time!"

Back at the brickworks Stefan said not a word to anyone of his adventure, not even old man Kostur. In any case, he was never asked where he had been.

twenty

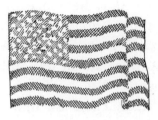

IN THE AMERICAN ARMY CAMP, WHERE STEFAN NOW
went in secret nearly every day to play the accordion,
there were no more than a dozen or so of Red Army
men. By their own choice they did not mingle with
the Americans. Though not all of them were Russian,
in the barracks among themselves they spoke only
Russian. Nevertheless, in their company Stefan felt
a kind of relief, as if, after a difficult striving, he had
arrived at some sort of destination that he was un-
willing to name to himself.

And this in spite of the fact that he did not particularly enjoy the company of the men. They were
a loud, rough lot and much of their talk among
themselves, over which they sometimes laughed up-
roariously, was quite over his head. At such times,
Stefan, eager not to be left out, only sat with an

empty grin on his face. This, too, seemed to amuse them sometimes.

Now and again, Captain Igor spoke to him of the people in the brickworks. He already knew a suprising amount about some of them, even named them by name, mentioned their birthplaces, their professions, and former places of work.

One day, he spoke of Mr. Behun. "Has he ever mentioned to you a colleague of his named Orest Kozak?" he asked.

At once Stefan was on his guard. He glanced at the captain. "No . . ." he said, looking away.

"Aha! Then ask him sometime and tell me what he says. And what about the man named Koval? You know him?"

In spite of himself, doubt must have shown on Stefan's face. The captain gazed at him for a moment; then, with a sudden rough movement, he pulled the accordion right out of his hands. "All right, kid," he said. "That's enough for today. Beat it!"

Sometimes Stefan found himself quite alone in their barracks. He liked that best; for, over the many months since he had left home, he found he had grown rusty on the accordion and being alone gave him a chance to practice without self-consciousness. He usually played for an hour or more, then made for the kitchen dump behind the camp.

By now, others from the brickworks had discovered the dump and whole families, swarming over it like

172

honeybees over a field of clover, foraged for food in it. Chicken feet and necks and even giblets could be found in the dump and these, when combined with fresh vegetables that were only partly wilted, made a delicious soup. For the children there were oranges only partly rotted and sometimes cookies and stale white bread. No end to the bounty of that dump!

Though Stefan made no secret of his visits to the dump, he said not a word to Mr. Behun or old man Kostur about his visits with the Red Army men. But trust Dr. Olha to notice something. One day, she said, "You seem more yourself these days, Stefko. I'm glad."

To his relief, she did not probe the matter further.

No one in the brickworks would ever believe that those visits of his were quite innocent. They would only be alarmed if they knew, even horrified.

Well, too bad! He did not have to answer to anyone any more. Besides, playing the accordion helped, just as Dr. Olha had noticed. It helped a lot. . . . Anyway, long ago, his father had promised him another accordion and this was how fate had chosen to fulfill that promise. It was no doing of his.

Yet, now and again, the perverse thought wandered into Stefan's head that he would have welcomed a reproach from Mr. Behun or Dr. Olha, or almost anyone else in the brickworks. Sometimes, he even yearned for someone to say him nay. But no one did, for he belonged to no one.

These days, people in the brickworks were not

concerned with how a lone boy spent his days. Instead, they kept a hawkish eye on the movements of the Americans for some clue, some hint of what they intended toward the thousands upon thousands of refugees from eastern Europe now in their hands. Dr. Olha was especially useful in this, because she frequently went to the Americans' D.P. camp nearby to look after some patients, and she kept her ears open for any news.

Then, one day, some families who had been staying in the D.P. camp stole away from it and moved into the brickworks. "The food's good," they said, "and it's free. But we feel safer here, especially now that Red Army officers have taken to visiting the camp."

"What are you saying?"

"It's true. They have been coming to visit each family in turn, trying to talk them into returning home. And the Americans don't—or won't—understand why we don't want to go."

A few days later came another piece of news, sending fresh shocks through the brickworks. Word spread that as a result of several visits from Red Army men to the American camp, three Russian families there had been persuaded to return home. At first this news perturbed people all over again. But when it was learned that the Russians were actually going home of their own free will, fears subsided.

"There's a place waiting for us," the Russians had explained, according to the report.

"Sure there is!" Mr. Behun exclaimed with a curt,

174

ironic laugh. "It's called Siberia. But for them," he went on, sobering, "it's not the same as it is for us. It's their own people that are in the saddle, and play the master in our land, too."

"True. But that regime of theirs wrongs them almost as much as it wrongs us."

Stefan listened in silence, then thoughtfully wandered out into the yard. He could not get them out of his head, those people who were going home. Though he had never laid eyes on them, they held an awesome fascination for him. At one moment, he looked upon them with dread, as one might upon someone condemned to hang. In the next, he felt sharp envy.

Truly, what was to become of him? Who was there to tell him? Not Mr. Behun who, in spite of everything that had happened, continued to treat him as a grown man. Not even Dr. Olha who, though she concerned herself with everyone's welfare, did so in a detached sort of way. What about old man Kostur then?

Stefan sighed. There was no one.

At last, as if he hoped to discover something from them, learn of some secret or talisman, he determined to visit the Russian families. So, early next morning, he set forth for the D.P. camp. On the way, he worried about getting past the armed guard at the gate. But when he reached there, some twenty minutes later, the guard only gave him a nod, and he passed through without even being asked for his papers.

As luck would have it, almost at once Stefan found

one of the Russian boys who was going home with his family. He struck up a conversation with him.

"So you're going home?" Stefan began.

A pained expression crossed the boy's face. "Well . . . yes."

"What's the matter? Don't you want to?"

"That's just it. I can't say. I do and I don't!"

Stefan laughed. "That's the way I am. But at least everything will be taken care for you when you get home. You won't have to bother your head about anything."

The boy nodded. "And we won't be alone, either," he said. "Others will be going with us. Tomorrow."

"From here? From the camp?"

"From here," the boy replied, "and from some other place, too. So they told us."

Stefan hung around the camp for an hour or more. Then, full of resolve, he left.

twenty-one

THE NEXT DAY, AS SOON AS EVER HE COULD GET away, Stefan made off for the American Army camp. On the way, he rehearsed what he would do. He'd draw Captain Igor aside, and say, "Listen, I want to go home, too, but my people are all dead and I have no one to go back to."

He knew for a certainty that, from then on, the whole matter would be out of his hands. And wasn't it better that way? Later, when everything was arranged, he'd go back for his things, say quick good-bys, and leave.

Reaching the camp, he saw an auto standing in front of the barracks where the Russians were quartered. A Red Army man, a sergeant, sat in the driver's seat, dozing. He looked up briefly as Stefan passed and gave him a nod of recognition.

When Stefan appeared in the doorway of the barracks, he was greeted by a chorus of glad cries from the dozen or so men inside. "Aha! Here he is! . . . Speak of the wolf and he's at the door! . . . Come in! Come in! We've been waiting for you!"

Startled by this unexpected welcome, Stefan paused on the threshold, a tentative grin on his face. They already seemed to know what he had come for; yet he had not told a soul.

"Come on! We have a little task for you! Just to suit you . . . a pleasant one!"

Stefan stepped inside. "What sort of task?"

"We want you to play the accordion for some friends of ours," Captain Igor said. "How about it?"

"Well . . . sure. Where are they?"

"We'll take you there. So go get the accordion and let's go!"

Elated, Stefan hurried to do as he was told. He'd speak to Captain Igor later. Having buckled on their side arms, Captain Igor and three of the others stepped outside, Stefan at their heels. To his surprise and pleasure, they led the way to the waiting auto.

"In you go!" said the captain, pushing Stefan into the seat next to the driver.

The driver watched as they all climbed in, then turned on the motor. "Okay?" he asked, looking around at them with a grin.

Okay!

Yes, it certainly was okay to be riding in this auto! Captain Igor leaned over and said something to the driver, who then looked at Stefan knowingly and nodded. Out of the corner of his eye, Stefan watched every move the driver made as they drove along. Some day, maybe, he'd be driving an auto himself!

So not until they had driven some distance did he realize that they were not going toward the center of town, as he expected. He began to wonder. Where were they going, anyway? He did not like to ask. But the farther along they drove, the more uncertain he grew.

Clutching the accordion on his lap, he had the sudden crazy impulse to open the door and leap out. He looked down at the asphalt road whizzing by. No, they were going much too fast.

He turned toward the men in the back seat, opened his mouth to speak, but before he could utter a word, Captain Igor cried, "Here we are!"

Stefan turned and looked. To his alarm, they were at the gate of the D.P. camp. What if Dr. Olha were there and saw him, big as life, in the company of Red Army men? But before he could decide what to do, the auto was waved swiftly through by the guard and came to a halt beside an open truck that stood in the middle of the compound. Numbers of people were standing about.

Before Stefan could make a move to jump out and make his escape, the captain, now with pistol in hand, was standing at the door, blocking it. "Stay where you are, kid," he said.

Stefan pushed the accordion off his lap onto the seat beside him. "But I don't want to . . ."

"Do as you're told," the captain ordered.

179

Stefan sank back into his seat. The driver now eased himself out and, leaning against the fender, stood placidly surveying the scene.

More and more people were coming out of the buildings and, while keeping their distance, stood about expectantly. Under their gaze, Stefan prayed for the earth to open and swallow him. Suddenly, a woman stepped out of the crowd and ran toward the auto. "Stefan! Stefan! What are you doing?"

Just as he feared. It was Dr. Olha.

The driver suddenly came alert. Whipping out his pistol, he took a step toward Dr. Olha. The crowd suddenly hushed. "Stand back!" he yelled.

Dr. Olha staggered and almost fell. "Stefan!" she screamed.

Then someone darted out of the crowd, caught her, and pulled her back. But she twisted around again. "Stefan!"

Stefan gazed at her, his eyes filled with sudden tears. Yes, now you care!

But at this very moment, all attention turned away from Stefan and toward the building from which the Russian families were beginning to emerge. Conducted by two of the Red Army men, pistols in hand, they started for the waiting truck. Each carried a bundle of his possessions, even the women and children. But neither of the army men made a move to help them with their burdens.

At last, Captain Igor turned toward Stefan. "Get out," he said, with a wave of his pistol. "Get out and start playing . . . something lively. And keep playing, no matter what!"

Stefan climbed out and reached for the accordion. Now, at last, they'd see that he was doing nothing evil, but only playing for the departing Russians. He adjusted the accordion and broke out at once into the liveliest polka he knew. At the sound, all heads turned and stared at him, open-mouthed, as if they had never heard an accordion before.

To the sounds of the gay music, in a ragged file the Russian families continued across the compound toward the truck. When they reached it, they were boosted up into it, one by one, and their baggage was thrown in after them. Ranging themselves along the guard rail of the truck, the families stood gazing back at the crowd. Several of the women were continually wiping their eyes with a corner of their head kerchiefs.

His fingers flying, Stefan played on without losing a note. The Soviet sergeant was again leaning at his ease against the fender, blandly looking on, his pistol dangling from his hand. The crowd stood motionless, as if mesmerized.

Stefan did not see that another automobile was now coming in through the gate. He did not notice it till it came to a stop almost beside him. In the front seat were two Red Army men.

And then Stefan saw who sat behind them. His fingers paused and the music faltered. Martin! And beside him sat his mother and Granny Sophia.

181

The captain gave him a sharp dig in the ribs. "Come on! Keep going!"

Mechanically, Stefan's fingers began to move again. As he stared at those in the back of the auto he was struck with the look of their faces, gray and curiously pinched. Martin was staring back at him, his lips moving almost imperceptibly, as if he wished to speak but could not.

One of the Red Army men now approached their auto and, lifting out their luggage, carried it to the truck and heaved it in. Stefan's fingers continued to move over the keys, his arms working the instrument.

And then, as he watched, with a sudden swift movement Martin covered his eyes with his arms. His mouth gaped open as if in a cry of anguish. The gesture was so sudden and so wholly unlike him that it made Stefan at last come to.

The cheap, grotesque music stopped in mid-note. In the dead silence, the accordion fell to the ground with a splintering gasp. For an instant, everyone stood still, waiting.

Then, suddenly, with a single leap Stefan reached the auto in which Martin and the two women were sitting and seized hold of the door handle. But before he could get the door open, Captain Igor had his wrist in an iron grip.

At this, the watching crowd at last broke loose and, with an angry roar, came surging at them. In another instant autos, truck, and men were engulfed in the yelling, shrieking crowd. Hands clutched at the doors, jerked them open, and reached inside for the occupants.

Sobbing now, Martin's mother and Granny Sophia fell into waiting arms. Shielded by the crowd, Martin and the two women were led away toward the barracks. Behind them, the rest of the crowd, howling, shaking fists, closed in on the Red Army men. Hands clutched and tore at their uniforms. Now, from various parts of the compound, American soldiers, bearing rifles, came on the run. But already the Red Army men had torn themselves loose, leaped into one of the autos, and started the motor. Plunging through the crowd, they shot for the gate and disappeared through it in a cloud of dust.

The Americans pushed back their helmets and stood staring, open-mouthed, after them.

Someone grasped Stefan by the arm. It was Dr. Olha. "Come, Stefan. You've done enough for today."

twenty-two

OLD MAN KOSTUR WAS ALL BUT BURSTING WITH IN-dignation. "Snatched right on the street, they were!" he cried. "Plucked right off the street and locked up!"

"Well, thank the good Lord they're safe now here with us," someone said.

"But that boy," put in another, "ought to get a sound thrashing! Him and his accordion!"

"Sh," old man Kostur said, "he's up there in his bunk."

"So what? He's not a child any more and ought to take thought!" That was Mr. Behun.

Stefan, lying face down in his bunk, listened.

"Wait a minute, sir," the old man said, "have you never made a mistake? The boy's on his own and made a mistake. Now he knows. And he's already ex-plained how innocently it came about."

"Maybe so. But these days innocence is a crime. Don't you know that, old man?"

Stefan's attention caught on that word and he lifted his head. Was he in truth innocent? But he was too miserable, too spent and wounded to search out the answer.

"Akh! Leave him be. He's wretched enough as it is."

Hearing these words, Stefan rested his head on his arm and, unseen by anyone, wept long and quietly. He wept for himself. He wept for his father . . . his mother. . . . He wept for everyone and everything. He wept for home, for everything lost. After a long while, still in his clothes, he fell into a deep sleep.

During the night, for the first time in many a month, he dreamed of his mother. She appeared to him as easily and clearly as if she were sitting there beside him. Her lips moved and she said something to him.

At that, he awoke with a start and sat up. For a long moment, he stared, motionless, through the window at the faint light of the coming dawn as he tried to recall what she had said in the dream. But her words had already faded away, along with the dream.

However, it did not seem to matter. Purposefully, as if some part of him had already come to a decision even while he slept, he reached for his pack and began to ferret about inside it. At last he drew out the cake of soap. He weighed it thoughtfully in his hand for a moment, then thrust it inside his shirt. Next, he took his identification papers out of his jacket pocket and put them in his pack. Better to be without identity. . . . Quietly, then, leaving the pack behind, he climbed down from the bunk and tiptoed out of the barracks.

Luck was with him, for he managed to cross the river and slip into the Soviet zone without mishap. Though the border was said to be well guarded, apparently the Soviets had not yet had time to set up barriers along the entire length of it, and there were still a number of gaps.

Guided by the landmarks that old man Kostur had remarked upon only a few short weeks ago on their way into the American zone, late that same afternoon Stefan reached his destination—the farm where his father and he had last stayed together.

Boldly he knocked on the door. When the master answered, somehow he did not seem as formidable as Stefan remembered him. "I've come for my father's valise," he said. He explained where it was.

At that, the man not only gave him permission to go into the barn to look for it, but even helped in the search. It did not take long. The valise was just where his father had hidden it.

Afterward, both the master and mistress urged Stefan to spend the night. Their son, they told him, had had to flee, leaving them to fend for themselves. They seemed pitifully cowed by the events that had turned out so disastrously for them. They welcomed Stefan as a partner in misery.

More than that, early the next morning when Stefan was preparing to depart, the master offered to drive him toward the border on his son's motorcycle. "They'll soon confiscate it, anyway, so we might as well have the use of it while we can," he explained.

That afternoon, when they made their farewells on a narrow dirt road skirting a forest, only a kilometer or so from the border, the master's eyes were moist. "God speed!" he said.

The moment he was out of sight, Stefan plunged into the forest. Burdened with the valise, he began the last and most hazardous part of his journey. If he were caught, the Soviets would never let him go, of course. They might even shoot him without asking questions first. And yet, though the valise was no less heavy than it had ever been, in place of the old resentment he began to feel a certain release.

Though going by way of the road would have been easier, Stefan prudently kept under cover of the forest, where numerous hiding places were only a leap away, should it come to that. The forest was silent. No bird called. Every leaf and branch hung motionless. All the forest was watching, breathless, to see what this wayfarer was about, how he would manage this dangerous journey that he had undertaken.

Stopping to rest for a moment, he sat down, his back against a tree trunk. It must have rained earlier, for the air was moist and smelled of the musky odor of fungus.

Glancing down and noticing the bulge in his shirt made by the cake of soap he had stowed there, he drew it out. He had brought it along to barter for his father's valise, but that had not proved necessary. As he held it in his hand, a voice said, "When you grow up, Stefko dear, we won't always be here to tell you what you ought to do, you know."

There. He had allowed her to say it at last.

"I know," he whispered. "I already know, Mama."

At last he got to his feet and started on again. Coming to a gully, he plunged down into it and on the other side hoisted himself out with the help of some shrubs growing along the rim. He set down the valise among the shrubs at his feet, and paused to catch his breath, alert for sounds of danger.

And then, just as he was reaching for the valise again, he heard it, behind him. A click . . . a single click.

He would know that sound anywhere. That was the sound that was always followed by the command, "Halt!" Or even, without further warning, by a pistol shot.

Too late to run. Slowly he straightened and, without turning, froze and waited. Waited for the sting in his back. The moment passed. Cautiously, he turned around. In front of him, not ten meters away, on the opposite rim of the gully stood a young man—hardly more than a boy—red star on cap, pistol in hand pointing straight at him. They stood staring at one another, motionless. At home, the thought at last came to Stefan, we would have been friends.

At some command within himself, Stefan held up the red-and-gold box of soap that he still had in his hand, so that the man could see it. It seemed to him then that the hand that held the pistol wavered a little. He tipped the box, slipped out the bar of soap, and wordlessly held it up. After a cautious moment, with a deliberate gesture that he hoped would speak his plea, he carefully placed both box and soap in full view on a bare spot, just on the rim of the gully.

Straightening, he exchanged a mute look with the soldier. The man nodded, then lowered his gun. Stefan turned and slowly walked away, all sensation concentrated on his back. As soon as he sensed that he was out of sight, he broke into a run. But he had gone only a few steps when he halted.

The valise. He had left it behind. In the urge to escape, he had completely forgotten the valise.

In despair, he dropped to his knees and for a long while sat there in a huddle. He couldn't go back . . . yet he must. For the sake of his father, he had to go back. Otherwise, all that he had gained would be lost forever.

A few minutes later, he approached the spot again. The young man had gone. The soap and its box were gone, too. The valise lay broken open, its contents scattered in the bottom of the gully. Scrambling down into it, hurriedly Stefan began to gather up all the papers and stuff them back into the valise.

My legacy, Stefan thought, as he recalled his father's words in referring to the contents of the valise. That meant a gift. His gift to the world. For some day, probably, the manuscript and the drawings would be published, and then anyone would be able to possess them.

Resting on his knees for a moment, Stefan gazed at the drawing he held in his hand. A delicate drawing of the feather grass, its long silken hairs waving in the wind, that each springtime once covered the boundless Ukrainian steppe land.

And now the real meaning of this gift came to him. It was not just the voluminous manuscript and the many drawings, done with so loving a hand. There was more to this legacy than that.

The manuscript and the drawings could not have been the work of a slave, but only of someone who valued freedom. For a moment Stefan paused to savor this illumination that had come to him at last so effortlessly. Why had he been blind till this moment? Well, no matter.

Hurriedly, he finished repacking the valise. He found the rope and tied it up again. Then, valise in hand, he started on. And as he made his way through the forest, he felt the presence of his father with every step he took. His long resentment was gone at last: he was rescuing the valise not for his father's sake, but for his own.

Fifteen minutes later, he knew that he was at last safe within the American zone, for there was the river. He crossed it and, in a few more minutes, came within sight of the smokestack of the brickworks. He set down the valise and heaved a sigh. He could afford to rest now. As he stood flexing his hand to ease the numbness, in the distance a lone figure swung into view. Stefan stood watching.

It was Martin. "We've been looking all over for you!" Martin called, running up to him.

Stefan looked at him. They'd been through a lot, both of them. They'd lived through the perils of war and had lost people most vital to them. They'd hungered and they'd wandered. They'd endured the same trials, without giving in. Because of all that, they would always understand the most important things about each other—and without any need to spell it out. That made them more than friends. It made them brothers.

"Let me?" Martin stretched out his hand for the valise.

Stefan nodded. "Careful," he said, "it's heavy."

They fell into step together. Behind them a jeep approached. It passed, then came to a halt just ahead of them. The driver, an American private, stuck out his head. "You fellas wanna lift to the brickworks?"

Martin looked at Stefan. Stefan smiled. "Okay!" he said.

Stowing the valise, the two boys climbed into the jeep and away they went past the greening fields.

About the Author

Marie Halun Bloch was born in Ukraine, and graduated from the University of Chicago. She worked briefly for the U.S. Department of Labor, but has devoted herself chiefly to writing, translating, and reviewing books for children and adults. Though *Displaced Person* simmered as a book idea for many years, Mrs. Bloch's final impetus to write the story came from a newspaper article she read about a Soviet-bred U.S. citizen who found difficulty accepting self-reliance as a positive value in American society. For the war background in this book, Mrs. Bloch drew on diaries and first-hand accounts of Ukrainian refugees in World War II. Mrs. Bloch and her husband live in Denver, Colorado and are the parents of one grown daughter.